The ASS
GOBLINS
OF AUSCHWITZ

CAMERON PIERCE

Eraserhead Press
Portland, OR

ERASERHEAD PRESS
205 NE BRYANT
PORTLAND, OR 97211

WWW.ERASERHEADPRESS.COM

ISBN: 1-933929-93-6

"Slaughter the shits of the world. They poison the air you breathe."
      - William S. Burroughs,
            The Place of Dead Roads

"Evidence flows up and down the dung shoot."
      - Paul Celan, *Flashlights*

Chapter One

The morning siren screams and the barracks come alive.

Otto and I crabwalk to the foot of the bunk and step onto the cold floor. Around us, children leap from their wooden beds. Since mine and Otto's ribcages are attached, sharing a bed is nothing new to us. Sleeping together is not what makes Auschwitz a living heck.

Smothered by other children, we swarm out the door and enter the icicled hallway. Blisters on my feet pop and freeze with every step.

At the end of the hall, light filters down from above. By now, Otto and I are adept enough at climbing the disintegrating staircase that connects our barracks with the rest of Auschwitz. We also know better than to be the first children outside. Everyone knows better, but every single day, someone gets marked for sacrifice. Today it's a toddler named Willow. She has been coughing and fainting all week.

The hazy glow of the rising sun creeps over me. I close my eyes. Somewhere to my right, Willow cries until the crackle of her legs splitting in a game of chicken bone smothers everything. Every morning, two ass goblins tear apart the first kid out of the bunkers. I learned not to look a long time ago.

An ass goblins shouts, "Apple!"

Everyone hustles to find their place in line so that we can march onto the marble apple patter in perfect formation. With thousands of children imprisoned in Auschwitz, this is just one impossible task we face every morning as we brush off the nightmares and vermin.

"Apple!"

Adolf used to conduct roll call, but he disappeared after my first week. Now the ass goblins seem to assign each other duties based on who loses in their nightly games of gambling. Without a staunch ruler, the order of Auschwitz is decaying. These days, the ass goblins only want to drink and make us build toys.

"Apple!"

Although Otto and I are conjoined twins, the ass goblins assigned us numbers 999 and 1001 when they stamped us into the camp records. I am 999, 1000 is a skeletal mute, and Otto is 1001. I never call him by his number, although he calls me by mine. He rarely speaks these days.

We spot 1000 and push through the crowd until we reach him. Fortunately, the flesh covering our ribs has receded so much that 1000 fits into the joint hollow of our bodies like a baby bird.

"Apple!"

The now-orderly line snakes between surgery quarters, gunnery towers, and Toy Division. Finally we arrive at the apple platter in the center of Auschwitz Square.

We step onto the apple by the stem. In a few hours, we will exit through the bottom. We serpent-march until all prisoners are in place, unless the ass goblins grow impatient and go S.S. on us. S.S. is short for Shit Slaughter. Shit Slaughter is the worst sort of punishment.

Otto, 1000, and I stand somewhere near the center of the platter. From the apple's bottom, an ass goblin calls, "Attention! Pants down, asses up!"

We drop our red camp trousers at the same time as all the other children, raising our butts toward the sun.

For many of us, this is the most dangerous part of the day. If you survive roll call, you notch it off as another day survived. New children might be at highest risk. Living by the rhythm of your own death sentence is a difficult thing to learn.

In an outer row of the spiral, a child blubbers his final words. *Toys mean freedom*, then the spluttering of slit vocal cords. The idiot. He was picked out of the litter to be today's apple. Did he really think spouting a goblin slogan would get him off the hook?

After the initial sacrifice, the apple is usually the second victim of the day. He or she is added to the cider vat, where they will ferment with the apples of previous days. Nobody knows how the ass goblins select the apple, but we suspect it has something to do with the ripeness of our assholes.

Frost lines my rectum by the time the roll call guard reaches us. I hold my breath and bite my tongue as a fat finger carves a swastika into the scar tissue of my left butt cheek.

The finger rockets up my dark zero. I bite deeper into my tongue. I seal my lips together, fighting the pain, ignoring the finger, and trying my best to remember that I am lucky because I am alive. Blood fills my mouth and drains down my throat, but I mustn't cough. The slightest peep means execution.

Plop! The finger pulls out. The ass goblin marks my number on the roll call sheet. He moves on to 1000, gives him the same treatment.

The pain of my tongue and ass prevent me from passing out. I exhale and gasp for air after the guard inspects another twenty rectums. Poor 1000 shivers against Otto and I. We are relatively safe for now. Bloody frost cakes my butt.

The ass goblin reaches the center of the spiral. Only the apple died during today's roll call, a rarity.

"Pants up! Eat breakfast!"

I pull my pants to my waist. Everyone else does the same thing. We disperse for breakfast only to discover that 1000 is frozen to our ribs. Otto and I shove at him, but he's stuck. Unwilling to be separated from the herd, we drag him toward the mess hall in the snow as naturally as temporary triplets can manage.

Chapter Two

At the far end of the mess hall, ass goblins stand onstage strumming stringed instruments and pounding on drums. These instruments are made of child bones and innards. I may have crafted one of them in Toy Division.

A painting of Adolf collects dust on the wall above the stage. Adolf looks almost identical to all the other ass goblins. He wears the same brown uniform, swastika armband adorning each sleeve, pimpled, plague-ridden ass sagging over his thighs. His ass is the biggest part of his body, no different than the ass of any other ass goblin.

His mustache sets him apart. His mustache is twice the size of his skull. Whereas normal ass goblins have a mouth that takes up their entire face, Hitler's mustache takes up his.

And Adolf walks backwards.

And dresses backwards.

He stands backwards in the painting.

No goblins have noses, which is how they fart up the earth without ever noticing. Their eyes hang from long, scaled stalks that jut out of their butt cheeks. In the painting, a cloud of yellow perspiration floats around Adolf's mossy skin. Other ass goblins consider him the purest and most perfect being on the planet. At least, they did until he disappeared.

Our trio mechanically gravitates to the nearest available table. We sit down and dig into the hill of dried skin piled in front of us. I reach for a face and the girl beside me slaps my hand. I punch her and tear the face from its boneless, meatless husk before she can react. I hold the face up to my own, peering through the eyeholes. I sink my teeth into the crusty lips. The lingering salt stings my tongue. Dried saliva liquefies in my mouth. Saliva drops are tasty, but I waste no time sucking them down. I'm starved, and we won't eat again until nightfall. Plus, there's a slight chance that the girl will risk attracting the guards' attention and try to steal this face from me. Faces are the most digestible part of a child.

I slide the nose over my bottom lip, forcing myself to swallow the cartilage without chewing, but I still taste some dead kid's bittersweet boogers.

I feel 1000 separating from my ribs. I look to my left just long enough to see that he is finally unfrozen. He breaks free from Otto and I. We're fortunate that the cider vats sit in the underground chamber beneath the mess hall. The rising heat makes it a lot hotter in here than outside.

I eat the face until only a strip of skin around the eye sockets remains. Whenever I get a face from the pile, I always leave this part for last. This way, I can make sure that I am not looking at anyone else while I eat. If you're suspected of looking at another child, even if they're thirty tables away, the ass goblins might accuse you of conspiring.

The band slams on their instruments. Over a discordant melody, they shout the mantra that hangs in neon over the main gate of Auschwitz. "Toys mean freedom! Toys mean freedom! Toys mean freedom!"

This means breakfast is over. It is time to work. It is time to build toys.

10

Chapter Three

I tilt my mouth toward Otto's right ear as we shuffle out of the mess hall. "What did you eat?" I ask. Black swastikles flutter to the ground.

Otto rarely says a word before breakfast or after work, so this transition period is my sole opportunity to speak with my brother. He's silent, shedding pounds . . .

"The ass goblins forbid conversation between workers."

. . . shrinking and shrinking . . . a five and a half foot dead baby.

"What did you eat, Otto?"

He says nothing and jerks away from me, but we're attached. There's no escape.

"C'mon, I'll tell you what I ate if you tell me."

"999, I will report all dissidents."

"You wouldn't report anyone, not your own brother. You would go down with me, don't you forget that."

We stand in line at the work assignment station and wait our turn. The line moves fast. Each child takes a card and reports to the Toy Division factory written on it, unless they are assigned to the surgery ward. The ass goblin dispensing the cards always gives Otto and I separate ones despite it being impossible for us to be in two places at once. Even Adolf made that mistake. Maybe it's an oversight on their part. Maybe we're the unknowing subject of an experiment, our every action observed and recorded until the day the doctors come for us. Most conjoined twins never sleep a night in the barracks. They go straight to the scalpel.

I hold the card right up to my eyes and squint at the scrawl. Today, I am supposed to report to the surgery ward. This has never happened to me. The surgeons are death doctors. Otto glances at his card and tugs me along. "Where are we going?" I ask.

He holds up his card. I strain my eyes, but it remains blurry. I can't read it. "Tell me what it says."

"The bicycle factory."

"Shouldn't we go to surgery? That's what I pulled, and you know what the scientists do to kids who ditch out."

"I must report to the bicycle factory and fulfill my duty as a worker. Go where you want."

I sigh. Otto is like a robot these days. I'm worried about him, and worried what will happen when the ass goblins realize they're missing me in surgery. They seem to find out every time. The kids who play hooky from surgery always disappear, but I know nothing more than rumors. Otto and I have never entered the surgery bay.

I wonder where Frannie got assigned, and if I'll see her tonight. She used to sleep in the bunk below Otto and I, but her twin has insisted that they sleep in faraway beds for the last three nights, which isn't fair at all. Frannie 2 is attached to Frannie's bellybutton and is no bigger than a doll. She shouldn't get to tell Frannie what to do. "I have to poop," I say, trying to forget her, thinking about my body's needs for once.

"Hold it," Otto says.

Are my eyes are as red and bugged out as his? We're both lice factories, that's for sure.

The sun is up and scaly cockrats scurry from their hiding places to scavenge for polar snakes. I wish we could eat them, but the ass goblins feed the cockrats and other creatures so much radiation that consuming animals is suicide. An easy suicide, I remember.

To get to the bicycle factory, we return toward the barracks, passing the apple platter in Auschwitz Square and descending a stairwell between the doll factory and the music factory.

Rumor says the entire underground of Auschwitz is dedicated to bicycles. It's supposed to be a maze of loops and tunnels and hills where ass goblins cycle, their favorite pastime. Frannie told me. She has no way of knowing, and she also told me that kids who survive long enough, well, they evolve beyond childhood and start looking like ass goblins. Frannie admitted she would have killed herself if she couldn't make up stories in her head. These must be some of her stories.

Even before we reach the bottom of the stairs, egg-shaped fart bubbles stink up the air. I cough into my hand.

Otto presents his work card to the ass goblin at the door. The goblin waves both of us in and slurps from a cider mug. Most twins—even non-conjoined twins—vanish shortly after entering Auschwitz. The Frannies are the only other pair to work in Toy Division for so long. Maybe we survive because ass goblins are always drunk and liable to make a few mistakes despite thinking they are perfect, or maybe Adolf was saving us for a special project before he vanished. I hope it's not the latter. I do not want to be special.

We find our place in a manufacturing line and set to work. Most children get assigned to the bicycle factory. A lot of bikes have to be built every day because they fall to pieces under the weight of the goblins' asses.

Today, Otto and I blow children's bladders into tubes and fit them into tires made of brains. Many brains go into each tire. Children near the beginning of the manufacturing line pull the brains from a vat and sculpt them into tires, making some fat and some skinny because ass goblins like a variety of bikes. I prefer making tires to filling and fitting tubes, but trading duties is forbidden.

I lean over the conveyor belt, careful not to brush up against the spinal frames, arm handlebars, or skull and foot seats that are beginning to pass by. I lift a bladder out of a barrel, feeling like my own bladder might explode any second. I blow air into a pre-slit end. After it's tight with pressure, I remove a brain tire from a different barrel and fit the tube into the jellylike groove. I drop the tire onto the belt and repeat the process a second time. I repeat it again and again, hour after hour.

Sometimes, I think the ass goblins chant my name as they ride bicycles, but they are only laughing. I no longer know my real name.

14

Chapter Four

Supervised by the eyeballs bulging out of goblin asses, we eat dinner in the bathroom, one floor below the barracks. "Asses down!" a goblin shouts.

Everyone drops their pants and plops down on a hollow tree stump that leads somewhere far below Auschwitz, maybe to the bicycle labyrinth. The ass goblins let us eat breakfast the child way, but they force us to eat dinner like them. With our asses. They flash yellow teeth at us, their grins widening to fill their entire faces. Watching so many children sit on toilet stumps makes them happy as heck. The band starts up with a detuned lullaby and all the goblins raise their quarts of cider, spilling everywhere. "Bring on the toads! Bring on the toads! Bring on the toads!" they chant. And they chug, chug, chug.

After breakfast and work, we end the day with toilet toads, creatures who live in the stumps and only emerge when summoned by the music of the ass goblins.

Inside my stump, a toilet toad croaks. Otto's toad croaks too. Here they come. I dig my fingers into soggy wood and hold on for dear life.

Slap! A tongue slips inside my rectum. Far longer than a goblin finger, the tongue wriggles all the way inside me and swims around my belly. Fed only the skin of children, there's nothing inside me for the toilet toad to grab, so it wedges another vital organ from its place. The pain differs from night to night, depending on what the tongue decides to pull from my body. Tonight is the worst kind of pain, my insides flaring up like I'm full of a thousand long knives.

I scream. Tears clean some ash from my cheeks. The ass goblins do not care how much we cry during dinner, so long as we plant ourselves to the tree stumps and let the toilet toads do their work.

My ass cheeks swell out as the tongue stretches my rectum wide enough for a large organ to plop out. Blood and feces gushing out, I focus on bracing myself to the stump. This is the point where some kids fall into the toilet, never to be seen again.

Then it's over, at least the first part. The toilet toad squeezes around my rear and hops into my lap. Toilet toads always melt a bit, as if they're made of chocolate. They're shit, though. Pure shit.

The toad wags its tongue, presenting me the pulsing red blob that it stole from my body. You never know what you'll be eating for dinner until this point. Tonight it's my heart. "Eat! Eat! Eat!" the ass goblins chant, relishing the festival of child misery.

I glance over at Otto. Apparently he'll be eating a kidney. "It's alright," I tell him, "I ate one last night. They taste better than the rest."

He glares at me, his eyes gray and his face in shadow. He unwraps the toad tongue and raises his kidney to his thin lips, takes a bite.

I take my heart in my hands but get caught up watching Otto. He smiles for the first time since the ass goblins took us from Kidland.

16

"Eat! Eat! Eat!"

Otto spits a kidney stone. The toad on his lap snatches it up and disappears between his legs, down into the tree stump. I didn't even know Otto had kidney stones. Maybe that's what has upset him so much. I hope he feels better now.

The toad sitting on me slaps my face three times in a row, smearing bile. I wipe the back of my left hand across my lips, but the toad slaps me again. The toilet toad is forcing me to eat with my lips covered in coppery-sour fluids. Best to finish fast. Fortunately my heart is small. I swallow half in one bite. Chew, chew, chew, vomit rising in my throat, chew some more, swallow. Satisfied, the toilet toad returns to its home. Subdued by agony, I choke down the second half.

The ass goblins stagger through the bathroom to ensure that every toilet toad is gone and that all children have eaten their dinner.

A few stumps down from Otto, a little girl holds something bloody in her hands. My vision is bad, but I know the mystery meat is supposed to be her dinner. She might be newer to Auschwitz. New kids usually have the most trouble stomaching their own organs.

I grip my stump, hoping this girl will just eat it. She still has time. The ass goblin inspecting our row moves slow and looks incredibly drunk. She needs to stop crying and stay strong. She doesn't understand. I would yell at her, but I am not the type who sacrifices his own hide for strangers. No heroics here.

The ass goblin reaches the girl and hoots loud enough for everyone—ass goblins and children alike—to fall silent and watch. The hoot of an ass goblin sounds very similar to a trumpet, an instrument I used to play. When an ass goblin

17

hoots, you know Shit Slaughter is coming. Apparently, this girl never caught on. She shoves the meat into her mouth. Her cheeks balloon out. The goblin scratches its ass and punches her in the throat. The meat flies across the bathroom, splattering across a boy's face. The girl wheezes and gags.

The ass goblin hoots a third time, jaws widening so far apart they unlock and fold over its head . . . row after row of rotten teeth.

"Shit! Slaughter! Shit! Slaughter! Shit! Slaughter!" the ass goblins chant.

The goblin picks the girl up by the throat. Her face turns blue. Vomit dribbles down her chin as the goblin takes her in both hands, turns her upside down, and shoves her up his own ass.

He jiggles from side to side and waves both sets of claws in the air. Egg-smelling steam burbles from his mouth. The ass goblins stop chanting. The big moment is almost here.

A swastika made from the little girl blasts out of the goblin's head, flinging shit as it spins around the bathroom and bounces off the walls. The goblin in Shit Slaughter mode bumbles after the swastika. After a pursuit that makes my head spin, his head of teeth snaps shut around the former girl, grinding her up. The ass goblin's head returns to normal. Dinnertime is over.

The ass goblins hardly pay attention to us during the ascent from the bathroom to our barracks. I must not be the only child who dreams of taking advantage of their drunkenness, but fear outweighs everything else. They go S.S. far more often at night.

Only one ass goblin watches over each barrack. After counting off two children in every bunk and turning out the lights, they lock the doors and drink cider with the others on night duty, usually checking in once every hour.

Otto and I climb onto our bunk and lie on our backs. Every muscle in my body aches. Tonight, I will force myself to rest. Besides Otto, Frannie is the only kid who has talked to me in Auschwitz. Now, in different ways, both of them are gone. One vanished into silence, the other into nowhere.

The lights go out. I am already fading when someone pinches my leg. "Otto?" I whisper.

"It is me, 999." he says.

"What's wrong?"

"I am afraid."

"I'm afraid too." I wonder if that's all he wanted to tell me, or if I should push him for more.

"They're going to separate us soon," he says.

"You don't know that," I say.

"I dreamt it." Otto tilts his head away from me. We sleep as far away from each other as our shared ribs allow.

I cry until I shit my pants.

I stopped dreaming when we came to Auschwitz.

Chapter Five

The bones of a cockrat lie in 1000's roll call nook. The vermin's meat has disintegrated into a sticky, umber muck that stains our flesh. I pry my fingernails beneath the radiated bones, but they do not budge. Cockrats are the real sentries of night. If you sleep soundly, even for an hour, they leap onto your bunk, snuggle close, and die.

Otto stirs with the morning siren. He punches the cockrat, bruising our joined part. "Why'd you do that?" I say.

"Say goodbye to 1000," he says.

We scamper out of bed and up the stairs, into a curtain of windblown swastikles. The sacrificial lamb is picked from the litter, breaking the bloody seal of another bloody day.

We drop our trousers and bend over on the apple platter. I try watching Otto, wondering if he truly believes that 1000 will be today's apple. Otto catches me keeping an eye on him and bares his teeth. 1000 fidgets between us. I squeeze my eyes shut, shut down my mind, and wait for my turn with the finger.

A claw carving another swastika into my flesh, the familiar prodding finger. I am seeing this from above, feeling none of the pain my body feels. I am floating above the crown of the ass goblin's skull. I must be very small. I realize that by will alone, I have shut down my mind. It's so easy to fly.

The finger no longer plugs my rear, but I am in my body again, and in pain. The ass goblin inspects 1000, taking a lot longer than usual. The ass goblin hoots. 1000 is bawling. I'm about to raise the floodgates myself, knowing I'll be at the zero point of a Shit Slaughter.

False alarm on the S.S.

1000 is today's apple, future cider of Auschwitz.

1000's killing freaks me out. I try not to mind that I get nothing more than foot skin for breakfast, but cheese blisters hardly soothe your nerves when some chicken butt who has hidden in the cavity of your ribcage for so long suddenly bites the dust.

"What do you think?" I whisper to Otto.

He stops chewing on some girl's face. "We separate ourselves. Before the ass goblins have a chance. We hide away bicycle parts until we can build a tandem bike."

I choke on a toenail.

Chapter Six

I am assigned to the surgery cathedral again. Otto is assigned to the doll factory. I show him my work card. "Two days in a row," I say. "They must be catching on."

"Speaking to other prisoners is prohibited, 999," my brother says. Apparently he's switched back to rule-following mode.

We march toward the doll factory without speaking. Around us, ass goblins ride bicycles. They catch oily swastikles in their mouths. Every day, more and more children fall down and never stand up. Every day, things get so much worse. The Auschwitz population dwindles as toy production rises.

Winter is heck. No sunshine illuminates our organs as they ferment in barrels, and later, after the cider is drunk, no sunshine warms the ivy lacing through our bones. We endure it to pay off the debts of youth, but we will never reclaim those happy times. Our punishment goes without cause or redemption.

Otto knocks on the door of the factory. We stand with our hands folded behind our backs until an ass doll opens the door. The ass doll waves us inside. Red semen-worms slither up the doll's nose. The doll shakes all over until the worms blast out of her rectum.

I hate the doll factory. We'll build dolls long into the night while ass goblins plug them hot off the assembly line. We make ass dolls in the likeness of goblins, but there are a few key differences. Each doll has a giant nose on its face rather than a fanged mouth. Like the goblins, their torso is a giant ass, but being legless, they also have a lower ass. All of them share Adolf's face, only their faces are made from rotten apples and have a nose behind the mustache. Like snow people made of children.

I used to fantasize that someday Otto and I would plug Frannie and her tiny twin the way goblins plug dolls, but today the idea disgusts me. Yolky fart bubbles stink up the air as goblins flop from doll to doll, playing musical chairs with the worm-spitting anuses.

No one stands guard in this factory, but misbehaving children still get caught. More than anywhere, asses really surround you here. Otto and I hopscotch between writhing dolls and goblins, making our way to the manufacturing line. No other children have arrived yet, so we take the first station, where we sculpt Adolf heads out of mushy apples, then attach the mustache. Despite knowing that the apples were once children, I believe most of their life essence drains out during fermentation, so sculpting heads isn't as bad as the other stages of doll construction.

Other kids arrive and find a place in line. Although we hate the job, we are all responsible for bringing ass dolls to life.

Hours pass. They whimper into other hours, as if time works independently of our crooked hands to animate the dolls. But

23

if our hands stop working, the assembly line will also stop. When you recognize that power, you cease being a slave to time. From that instant onward, you are a bastard slave. So much for epiphanies.

Eventually, two sentries come for me. Otto drops a mustache on the floor and they beat us until we throw up.

"Missing in surgery," they say. "Guilty, guilty!"

I rest my head on the mustache and begin counting down from nine hundred ninety-nine.

On my thirty count, they nail our hands to a wooden surgeon's table. At zero, they hammer into our feet. Otto and I sputter blood and shit as the sentries announce the punishment we are to be dealt: Revocation of Childhood by Molecular Entropy for the Advancement of the New Order. The guard reading this bumbles and slurs over every word. He obviously has no idea what it means, and neither do I. They leave.

An ass goblin in a full-body plastic suit enters the operating theater. Beneath the suit, the goblin appears to be white. This is strange, although considering that Otto and I may never face another roll call, it is not so strange. The prospect of dying exceeds all other absurdities.

The goblin in plastic turns his back and fiddles with something on a counter. He turns, and a swastika-shaped needle enters my arm.

I am not around for what happens next.

Chapter Seven

"Wake up!"

My eyes are already open when I return to consciousness. An ass goblin stands over me. I try turning my head to check on Otto, but my skull won't budge from the icy table. All I see is the ass goblin in the plastic white coat, spreading his arms wide. His hood is down now.

"Beautiful! Marvelous!" the goblin says. "Bumblestum, come quick. Examine this child. The skin grafts are taking hold better than I've ever seen."

This is the first time an ass goblin has referred to another by name in my presence. I realize that all of them must have names. Adolf is not alone.

An elderly ass goblin gets on a stepladder beside the table and raises his wrinkled, semi-deflated ass to my face. "You are correct. These skin grafts are splendid, eons ahead of anything else in the field. How is the other twin doing?"

"What have you done with my brother?" I croak.

Bumblestum expels a gas cloud into my face, dazing me into yellow nausea.

The ass goblin in the white coat sighs. "For the first several hours, 1001 demonstrated remarkable external healing. I believed I had found what we've been looking for. All the while, 999 was dying. I am at a loss to explain what happened next. 999 made a comeback, reconfiguring a fraction of his DNA structure, just enough to survive, while the life force drained from 1001."

"Now that's science!" Bumblestum says.

"Although it is policy to dispense of twins post-surgery, I believe 999 and 1001 bear great potential for the scientific community. They have survived better than many children since their arrival, potentially destroying Adolf's theory that twins, especially conjoined twins, are inferior to the single-type child."

"Adolf is not a scientist, but if our research disproved any of the rational arguments he laid out in Mein Puppe, Auschwitz could lose its science division, and we would lose our asses."

"The odds of Adolf returning are slim. I anticipate taking full charge of Auschwitz by morning. It will be the dawn of the renaissance we've been fighting for." The goblin in the white coat smiles. The overhead lights reflect off his flesh, making him look shiny and beatific, a white angel.

"Auschwitz will be a great kingdom . . ."

The White Angel nods. "Tonight, I'll return them to the barracks and begin the study on their post-conjoined lives."

Bumblestum hops off the stepladder, clapping and giggling. "Genius! If we remake children in our likeness, we will be *so close* to discovering a viable childhood serum. This could be the greatest leap forward in ass goblin evolution since the invention of ass dolls."

The White Angel's eye stems elongate from his ass as he pokes and prods my body. "Nay, it is greater. After we acquire innocence and youth, our race will be unstoppable.

We will become immortals."

For the most part, I am numb. I imagine this is how it feels to be dead . . . tingling feet and a desire to puke.

The ass goblins turn off the lights and exit the room.

Chapter Eight

The White Angel takes me to the barracks after lights out. The ass goblin who is supposed to be holding post outside the door waddles over from a card game with the other guards. "Just a game of gambling," he explains, his eyes peeping out from his fat buttocks, staring guiltily up at the scientist.

"I am only returning a prisoner," the White Angel says. "No need to be alarmed. Doing my duty, as you do yours."

He scales the staircase two steps at a time, leaving me alone with the guard. His gambling buddies holler at him. Some want him to return, others drunkenly clamor for a wee hour Shit Slaughter. "Ah, forget it. You got the mark of a hot one." He unlocks the door, pushes me through, and locks it behind me.

I hold my breath in the darkness. Children whisper in their bunks. My entrance must have startled them. My vision isn't adjusting, so I grope along from bunk to bunk until I find the eighth on the wall to my right. That is where Otto and I slept. I run my hands against the side, calculating the easiest way to pull myself up. My right hand brushes against something cold and small. I slide my fingers over each of its sides and realize that I have discovered a foot. The foot's owner jerks away and I leap back. The foot owner sits up, leans close to me. "Who are you? What do you want?" she whispers.

I would recognize that whisper anywhere. It's Frannie. She's alive after all. "It's me," I say, my throat raspy and sore.

"Who are you?" Her eyes must be closed. They aren't flashing in the dark like they used to.

"999, Otto's twin."

"Oh . . ."

Someone stirs beside Frannie. The form pushes Frannie down on the wooden cot and creeps to the end of the bunk. I fail to make out the face until sour breath curdles my nostril hairs.

It's an ass goblin. Frannie is sleeping in my old bed with an ass goblin.

"999," the ass goblin croaks, "it is Otto, your brother."

I grab hold of the cot to keep from collapsing on the floor, and in one unbearable moment, it all comes rushing back to me. I understand the meaning of the conversation between the White Angel and Bumblestum after our separation.

"I am not an ass goblin," he says, his voice totally ruined. He couldn't speak above the softest whisper if he tried. And neither could I.

"I'm sorry I let you down," I say. "I'm sorry for cutting us apart. I messed up our entire plan. We'll die here for certain now."

"Your eyes are weak, but in the morning, you will see that we can no longer pass as children."

"What's to be done about this?"

"Climb into bed. The morning siren should be sounding soon. We must rest until then."

Otto slides his hands under my arms. Claws he never

had before dig into my back as he lifts me onto the bunk. I push Frannie into the middle, between Otto and I, and pass into a dream about plugging her miniature twin, my first Auschwitz dream.

Chapter Nine

No matter how many times it startles me, I am never ready for the morning siren. Today seems worse, probably because nobody's condition ever improves in Auschwitz. It's a lemming-drop straight to the bottom. I am also recovering from surgical procedures not yet familiar to me. I gaze sleepily at Frannie and Otto. He is sitting up in bed. She is also sitting up in bed, but missing her head. Her torso is a pair of lips. We have no time to discuss her headless condition, for the guard at the door is eager to clear the barracks, swiping his claws at children as they scuttle into the hall.

Green claws twice the size of my hands are grafted to my skin. My palms look normal, as do my arms and legs. I pat my butt and that seems regular too. Even if I am no longer a pure child, at least I do not have a goblin ass.

I run to catch up with Otto, leaving Frannie behind in the crowd. The less contact she and I have beyond the barracks, the safer we will be.

Today is the coldest of the season. Swastikles blow in on a southbound gust. Thunder and lightning gallop across the horizon in fits and starts. I can hardly make out the ass goblin's cry of "Apple! Apple! Apple!" This is going to be one heck of a roll call.

I catch up to Otto as he seeks out his usual place in line. The chaotic weather disrupts our natural order. Bewildered goblins poke their heads out of factories or pace around the apple platter. Unless they're assigned roll call or breakfast duty, few ever show their heads until the work day begins. Big storms must affect their perfect alignment with the universe.

My first direct view of Otto almost makes me bite my tongue in half. I understand why I mistook him for an ass goblin in the dark. His child hands are gone. His new hands look to be green rubber gloves ten sizes too big. They hang down to his knees. A rubber mask has melted over his gray face. He catches my drop-jawed stare, his expression synthetic, unchanging. "You are not much better," he says.

Last night, I thought he could hardly muster a croak because of throat problems like my own, but the mask muffles his voice. I hope he can withstand these mutations.

"Attention! Asses up!"

We drop our pants. My brother's ass puffs out, a lunar nightmare of craterous pustules. Semen worms slither out of his infected tissue and dive to the apple platter. They burrow into the marble where 1000 used to cower. Nobody has replaced the cider boy.

My spine aches and threatens to crack in two by the time the ass goblin taking roll reaches us many hours later. The sun never rises.

I brace myself for the typical swastika carving and rectal inspection. The guard sets one hand on my buttocks and lets his claws linger. I try to leave my body. No success. I nearly pull off the flying trick when the guard's hand darts between my legs and tugs on my scrotum. Against my better judgment, I turn my head and catch sight of a needle.

The needle enters my right testicle. Barf and stomach acid rockets up my throat. I swirl it around in my mouth to keep from puking on the marble. I might already be in serious trouble for turning my head. The bile catches in the gaps between my teeth and congeals around my tongue. The needle drains my right testicle until the nut inside the sack shrivels to nothing.

I can't tell for sure, but the White Angel appears to give Otto the same needle treatment.

The snow turns to sleet.

When roll call ends, I rise into the black of night, my body crackling in a million different places. The White Angel orders us directly to the work assignment station. No kidskin for us today.

I pick bile from between my teeth with a clawed hand. Otto and I waddle side by side, rubbing our empty sacks. "Auschwitz is transforming," he says.

"We are the transformed ones," I say. "They want to remake us in their image. They want Auschwitz to be a fairyland."

Chapter Ten

The White Angel also controls work assignments tonight. He stands under a flickering bulb that sways in the wind. When Otto steps up, the ass goblin hoots. Rather than handing over the next card in the pile, he takes a blank slip from his pocket and scribbles on it. "Doctor's orders."

Otto shuffles away with his head down. The White Angel gives me a special note as well. I am to report to the bicycle factory. I slosh through the mud, catching up with Otto. "Let me see your card," I say.

He holds the paper out to me, but the ink has already smeared into black rivers. "Surgery," he says, "I am going to surgery." And then he is gone.

We have never worked a day apart in our lives.

I trudge on toward the bicycle factory. Other children scurry to their own work assignments. Even in the storm, many do a double take when they see me.

A few ass goblins stand beneath awnings, drinking cider. Some of them whisper and point when I pass.

I stand outside the darkened bicycle factory and shiver from scalp to toe. No lights emanate from the underground. I descend the stairs, scraping my claws against the walls to my left and right, calling, "Hello? Hello?"

No reply. I knock on the door.

Again, silence. I turn the knob. The door creaks.

My work slip is a soggy shred of runny ink, so if I encounter an ass goblin down here, I'm liable to receive a Shit Slaughter regardless of the White Angel's sudden takeover of our daily routine.

I shut the door behind me and move by memory toward the guard's corner. I swat at the air until I grab hold of the electricity pulley. I lower the chain. Gray lights dance around the room. They settle as the conveyor belt whirs alive.

I look around, paranoid that I am not alone. Assigning me to the bicycle factory could not be a mistake on the White Angel's part. He wanted me here. I am an experiment, a special project. A hated pet.

The ass goblins must be watching me, recording my actions. My instincts tell me to take advantage of this opportunity and go forth on Otto's dream of constructing bicycles to ride into the labyrinth. If this is a behavioral study, then rebelling against the ass goblins will result in death. They won't risk preserving a test subject whose foremost instinct is rebellion.

A red bulb combusts in the dusty core of my brain.

I run around the room, flailing my arms. I must find a bicycle . . . a bicycle that is already built! The ass goblins will condemn me for riding a bicycle into the labyrinth, but if I play it off as a genuine result of their genetic experiments, I might build intrigue and buy time.

Handlebars and half a wheel jut from a mound of bones. I raise my arms into the air, jiggle my fingers, and dig. The children whose bones and organs make up this bicycle, they're no longer the same. Neither am I. We all come to Auschwitz as children, but in the long run, we become something else . . . cider, bicycles, goblins, food for prisoners . . . dolls. Nobody remains a child.

I unbury the bike and wheel it to the guard's station. The rusted door in the back leads to the underground labyrinth. I prop the bike against the wall and turn the swastika handle.

The door swings open. Colored lights flash along two sides of a tunnel. Goblin laughter echoes from somewhere on the other end. I grab the bike and lift my right leg to mount it. Immense pressure builds in my ruined sack. I bite my tongue and pedal into the tunnel.

Chapter Eleven

I force myself not to depress the brakes at the end of the tunnel. That doesn't seem like an ass goblin thing to do, and maintaining appearances is essential to my survival.

It's a wise decision. Straight out of the tunnel, the trail plummets into three loops. Green and yellow lights swirl on the track. I hold on tight and pump my legs to gain enough momentum for the loop-de-loop-de-loop.

Upside down!

Right side up.

Upside down!

Right side up.

Upside down!

The trail splits two ways. The one I'm heading toward is a green spiral downward. I make a sharp left turn and take the yellow trail. Mist rises all around. Individual corn kernels comprise the squishy, bumpy road. The goblin laughter fades. Their bicycle labyrinth must be down the green path.

When the mist clears, I spot cockrats swimming in shallow canals that line the corn road. In front of me, a litter of cockrats dances after a cockroach bigger than an owl. I wonder what they're following it for.

I shift my eyes back to the yellow trail—
No time to brake. A brick wall blocks the path. I squeeze the handlebars, not skilled enough on a bike to maneuver a graceful fall. I close my eyes . . . and crash through soft bricks. The bike slips from under me and I go tumbling, landing in a pile of foam rectangles.

I pick up one of the black bricks, digging my claws into the soft sides. I drop the brick and stand. The bicycle drags itself toward me, shrinking smaller and smaller. The bicycle becomes my testicle, alleviating my scrotal pain. I pat the flesh-encased bicycle and carry on.

This side of the foam bricks, the corn kernels slowly diminish into warm chocolate cake. I sink up to my ankles in frosting. The yellow lights fade behind me, but holes of light on the ceiling guide my way. This is where the tree stumps lead. This is the lair of the toilet toads.

The walls that kept the path easy to follow cease. I decide that exploring the cavern is worth the risk of encountering a toad gang. This place almost seems untouched by the ass goblins. It's more like Kidland.

A hill appears on the horizon. Before moving on, I dig both hands into the chocolate cake. At first, I only lick at the frosting, remembering the sickly sweet richness.

I mash two heaps of cake into my mouth at once. Cake plugs my nostrils, crusts over my eyes, and dribbles down my face. The frosting is so thick and creamy that it lines my throat and cuts off my breathing. I roll onto my back. Frosting suffocates me from outside and in. I slap my hands against my cheeks and half-chewed cake torpedoes from my mouth. Gravity jerks it back and the spit-up cake splats across my face. I sit up, no longer choking. I resolve to ease up on the cake consumption.

Looking like a mucky frosting monster, I bound toward the hill. With today's tweaked schedule and the White Angel running the show, who knows when work will end tonight. I'll have to hurry. Now is not the time to go missing in action.

I realize what the hill is made of, and suddenly the cake tastes bitter. I wipe my hands on my trousers and tread over the dead kids at ground zero.

Chapter Twelve

I stand at the top of the hill and look out. The underground cavern is very bright from this vantage point. The walls appear to be chocolate cake, as penetrable and temporary as the floor. I think of Otto and sit down. Hopefully he is okay. You're lucky if you return from one trip to the surgeon's cathedral, and hopelessly lucky if you return from two visits.

This brings me back to the days in Kidland, when everyone lived happy and free. Older kids like Otto and I taught lessons in schoolhouses, but that was the limit of authority. After lessons, we played as equals with the students. Everyone got along and no one was ever bullied. We cooked communal dinners on grassy knolls, smoked dandelions, played games with lemmings and other creatures, and snacked on whatever fruit happened to be in season. I liked strawberries the most.

We were a city of children, then one day we became prisoners, though not all at once. They stole us from our tree houses in droves. Nobody left their quarters after word got around. The sun fell out of the sky. I remember staying up late one night after the raids began. I wanted to catch sight of our abductors. That was the night the ass goblins came for us. Reeking of skunk spray, two goblins bashed our faces and said, "Don't you cry." They put us in a boxcar crammed with children. In the dark I cried, "Who are they? What do they want with us?"

"Ass goblins," somebody said, "they live in a place called Auschwitz."

When the train to Auschwitz arrived and the doors were thrown open, Otto and I stumbled out. The sun reappeared. Sunbeams the color of algae touched our skin, but the light made us cold. It began to snow.

There's an unspoken rule in Auschwitz. We never speak of Kidland. As far as I'm concerned, nobody came up with this rule. Silence is an easier response to horror. It swallows up your memories. Sometimes, though, one is belched up from the blackness. I lie down on the hilltop and rest my left cheek in the palm of a dead girl. I look into her sunken eyes and say, "What do they want with us?"

It's just like before, only this time I have an answer. I reach out and touch the girl's lips. They're hardened into a smile, a hopeful thing. Children who died in Kidland always died smiling. I sit up and brush shavings of rot from my body. I think I will escape now. I won't find a better chance. I can burrow through the chocolate cake and get out of Auschwitz.

If I don't flee now, I'll reface the scalpel like Otto. My brother, eternally at my side until of late, and Frannie . . . our conversations meant the world when not even Otto spoke to me. Together, in their special ways, the two of them sustained my will to survive the daily trials. Leaving them behind, I would lose a piece of myself. I could never, but I have to . . . *Ribbit!*

Ribbit! Ribbit! Ribbit!

Toilet toads hop up Dead Kid Hill on every side.

I spin around, seeking out the best passage down the hill. They block all possible escape routes. Their tongues flail as they leap and crawl closer, inviting me to a personal death party in the lingo of amphibians.

The toads swarm as one fluid mass. The top of the hill no longer seems high up. I squeeze my bike sack and wonder if dying—the act itself—actually hurts.

Hot pressure builds in my scrotum as the toilet toads approach the top.

Their front line passes the halfway mark. They belch a unanimous rat-tat croak as the bicycle grows inside me, reversing its earlier shrinking process.

I hold the flesh-encased bike until my sack pops. Teeth grinding the pain away, I mount the bicycle and pedal like mad. I head in the direction of the loop-de-loop-de-loop because it serves as my sole chance of survival. The toads and I are set to collide three-quarters to the top.

I rear back on the handlebars. The front tire elevates. Afraid of falling, I lean forward and duck my head. Toilet toads gnash at the air as I soar beyond the reach of their tongues.

The rest of the journey down Dead Kid Hill through chocolate cake and up the yellow road blurs as adrenaline pumps the chewed pieces of my heart past overdrive.

Chapter Thirteen

The door to the bicycle shop is still open when I emerge from the underground. I twist the swastika handle and push on the door, ensuring that it is locked. Before I turn around, an ass goblin hoots behind me. "What are you doing here?"

"N-nothing."

"Nothing?" The goblin waddles toward me, brushing swastikles off its swastika armbands.

"My work assignment ordered me to the bicycle factory."

It points toward the door at my back and hoots a second time. "Did your work assignment order you through that door?"

I shake my head left and right. A gun sits on the counter of the guard station, out of the ass goblin's sight. I was too occupied to notice it before. Guns are so rare, it's easy to forget they exist.

"Are you Experiment 999?" the ass goblin says.

I nod and step up to the counter, resting my hands there as naturally as my nerves can muster.

The ass goblin charges. "No sudden movements!"

I grab the pistol, fire, miss. Fire and miss. Fire and miss. I close my eyes and fire. The gun clicks. I open my eyes. The ass goblin transforms into S.S. mode five feet away. Backed against the door, I raise my clawed hands, as if showing the Shit Slaughterer that I'm part goblin will save my scalp.

He swipes at my brow. I duck.

"Hoot! Hoot!" He swipes again.

I dodge to the left, but his claws rake across my chest. I crumple into a ball and tuck my head to my knees.

He kicks me in the stomach. I curl up even tighter.

The door leading to the rest of Toy Division opens wide. In steps the White Angel. "What's this nonsense?" he says.

"The prisoner entered forbidden quarters," the Shit Slaughterer says. He kicks me again.

The White Angel storms across the room and seizes the goblin by his jaws. After yanking out a handful of teeth, he shoves the goblin to his knees. "You do not reprimand my experiments," the White Angel says. "Consider this your final warning."

The Shit Slaughterer bows his head.

"Come, child," the White Angel says. He grabs my elbows and pulls me to my feet.

"Science awaits you."

Chapter Fourteen

"Tell me why I keep you alive," the White Angel says.

Chained to a chair, I stare at the paleface goblin, seeing double. Funhouse mirrors cover the walls, distorting the ass goblin and I. The mirrored ceiling reflects the swastika painted on the ground, twisting it around into a star.

"Do you remember when Adolf governed Auschwitz?"

"He vanished not long after we—I arrived."

"What do you remember about his reign?"

The rule of Auschwitz is that children should listen and never be heard, so I am unused to answering questions.

"Answer the question!"

"Children die now the same as before."

"I want to make Auschwitz the happiest place on earth."

"Then stop killing us, stop making us work."

"You will work no longer, 999. That is why I ordered the bicycle factory to be unoccupied when you arrived. I needed to understand what you would do, where you would go. Most ass goblins want you dead. They're afraid to watch you, a child, become one of them without losing the grace of childhood."

"One of them? But I'm not an ass goblin."

The White Angel ignores me. "Considering twins are more inclined to display psychic abilities, I might know just the trick to solidify my argument supporting your value as a test subject."

"I am not a monster."

"Not yet, at least. Your brother, on the other hand, finds himself in a radically different situation, thanks in part to your confrontation with the sentry, who insisted that some punishment be dealt. Retribution in the name of science is the greatest retribution. That is where Adolf and I disagreed. I am sure he would be pleased to learn that I punished your brother instead of you, the guilty one. If Adolf were still with us. . . but his ideas were ass backwards" The White Angel laughs maniacally. "Bring in the spider goblin!"

The wall straight ahead opens up. Two ass goblins drag a hideous creature into the room by heavy chains padlocked to its neck. I scream until the White Angel punches my nose. I pipe down, choking on blood and snot.

Otto, my brother, is no longer Otto. He cannot be Otto. Eight hairy arachnid legs hold his torso ten feet off the ground. His arms and legs are gone. Except for the spider limbs and goblin ass, bandages mask his entire body.

"Enough frontal," the White Angel says. "Show us that ass!"

The sentries march around the spider goblin like they're in a cakewalk. They spin Otto's rear toward me. An apple-sized eye blinks out at me from his rectum.

"I've always thought spiders were nature's freaks. They have too many eyes. With eight legs, a single peeper should suit your brother fine. He's an ideal prototype for arachnids of the future. He's spidery and gobliny, but childlike. The two of you are my greatest creations, and I'm only getting started. Take the experiments to Cell Eight and ask Stumblebum to prepare for the next procedure."

I scream that I do not want any part in this. The White Angel pats my head. I bite his hand. He thrusts a syringe down my peehole and injects a searing fluid, I guess to scold me. "You will be my perfect toy soldier," he says.

Chapter Fifteen

One year before . . .

Otto and I sat on one of the hills overlooking Umbrella Park, a mushroom-dotted area where kids pounded on drums in in a huge circle. Neither of us ever got the hang of drumming. My trumpet laid beside me, but I was too nervous to play. Frannie had been ignoring me for weeks. I planned to ask her about it tonight, after the drum circle ended and we met up for story time.

Otto's face was buried in a book. I lit up a dandelion, took a puff, and snatched the book away from him.

"Give it back, jerkface!" he said.

The cover featured a pirate ship full of lemmings wearing eye patches and baggy plaid pants. They raised swords to a skull flag. "Lemming Pirates Versus Japan?" I asked. "What's Japan?"

He took the book away from me. "Japan is a made-up place where kids enslave each other. The lemming pirates are going to Japan to rescue the slave children and turn Japan into a free world."

"That doesn't make any sense. No kid would ever want slaves."

"Leave me alone. It's just a story. Anyway, Frannie

recommended it to me."

"Liar." I exhaled dandelion dust in his face.

Otto closed the book in his lap. "It's true. She woke me up last night and gave it to me. She said I would appreciate it."

"I would appreciate it too."

"She said you wouldn't."

I picked up my trumpet. "I guess we should be heading to the campfire. I want to talk to Frannie before story time starts."

"Are you going to ask her out?"

"What makes you think that?"

"You've been talking about it forever. I don't think you should. She's annoying. Besides, she'll crush you like a bug. Remember how Leonard could never play board games after they went out last year? Leonard loved board games. He was a board game master," Otto said.

"Leonard was afraid of Frannie 2. What happened to him doesn't count."

The drums faded away as kids headed for story time. I blew a discordant melody into Otto's ear to let him know I was irritated. He covered one ear with the book. I started feeling bad and lowered the trumpet.

"I'm sorry," I said.

"It's just an all-around bad idea," he said.

We shuffled down the hill.

The dandelion crumbled and I pulled another from my pocket. I lit it and turned my gaze to the reddening sky. I thought that all the planets up there must be full of kids like us. Maybe Japan was one of those planets.

When we made it to the center of Umbrella Park, the last drummers were packing up their instruments. They passed dandelions and gave each other high fives.

"Great drumming," I said.

A girl smiled at me and said, "Hey, it's Detuned Trumpet Boy!"

A boy with long hair raised his hands and fingered an air trumpet. He made farting noises with his mouth. We laughed about it as we moseyed out of the park.

Otto and I walked near the back. A few toddlers thanked us for the lesson on making carnival costumes that we taught in the schoolroom that morning. "Tomorrow, you'll learn about scenery," Otto told them.

I was too preoccupied with Frannie and the planets to respond.

The group dispersed. Half of the kids went to their tree houses, the other half to the campfire. Frannie climbed down the ladder of her tree house and ran to catch up with us. "Hey! How's it going?" she said.

Otto held up the book. "I'm halfway through," he said.

Frannie glanced at me and then stared at the ground. Her cheeks reddened. "Guess what? Frannie 2 and I are telling a new story tonight."

"That's super awesome," I said. The Frannies told the best make-believe stories. "It's good we ran into you too. I wanted to talk to you about something."

"Oh . . . well . . . Frannie 2 and I really need to set up props for our story. Can we talk later?"

"Yeah, sure," I said.

"See you around!" Frannie waved goodbye before running off.

When she was out of sight, Otto said, "What do you like about her anyway?"

"She's the prettiest conjoined girl in Kidland."

"She'll spit you out and swallow you."

"It's none of your business what she does."

He touched the flesh that covered our connected ribs. "Everything that happens to you affects me equally."

After story time, the Frannies went off with the other storytellers. They vanished before I got the opportunity to tell them how much I enjoyed their tale. It was about a bird who met an alligator in Kidland's swamp. They fell in love and lived happily ever after. I felt bad that Frannie didn't even wait around to talk, but she was probably eager to celebrate with the other storytellers.

Otto and I tramped through the woods. We were a little too clumsy for rope ladders, so we had installed a pulley system that lifted us into our tree house.

We burned candles and smoked a few dandelions. I rubbed their feathery ashes into my palms while Otto played a spooky bedtime song on his pumpkin piano.

"Play your trumpet," he said.

I shrugged and picked up my trumpet.

Before I blew into the horn, spheres of light exploded in the sky, splitting the night at its seams.

We stood and rushed to the doorway. Out by the swamplands, flames washed over the forest. Otto and I looked at each other, both of us hoping the other would make some call to action.

"We should stay inside," Otto finally said.

So we pinned a blanket over the doorway, blew out the candles, and cowered in the dark. We were frightened and couldn't help but cry a little as kids screamed outside,

22

in the burning darkness.

"What do you think it is?" I said.

"I think Kidland is being invaded," Otto whispered. "Those were spaceships crashing down."

"What's *invaded* mean?" I lowered my voice as well.

He shushed me and took my hand.

Invaded must have been something he read about. It sounded really awful, judging by the nightmare sounds outside. And crazy too. Spaceships only existed in make-believe stories. I buried my head in his shoulder and broke down. "I don't want to be invaded," I sobbed. "I don't want spaceships to be real. All I want is Frannie."

He wiped snot from my nose. He pressed his slick hand over my mouth. The scariest laughter echoed across Kidland. He cried his head off, and the next few days passed in a blur of panic and whispered rumors.

Chapter Sixteen

I hang from a barbed hook in a large cell with the spider, my brother. He broods in a corner. Headless Frannie is there, and also a girl who looks identical to the old version of Frannie. It must be Frannie's twin, all grown up into a regular child. "Hey," I say, "can someone slide this hook out of my ass? I want down from here."

The cell looks cleaner and more comfortable than the barracks. Windows occupy most of one wall. Ass goblins stare in. I guess we'll be under constant surveillance.

"The White Angel told us not to take you down," Frannie says. She's completely naked. From the waist up, she's nothing more than a huge pair of lips with two arms hanging from the sides.

"Why not?" I say.

"He'll come for you when he's ready," she says.

"Is my nose still broken?"

"You don't have a nose anymore."

"No nose?" At least I can breathe fine, I guess. "How's Otto doing?"

Frannie purses her giant lips. "He won't speak to me."

I stretch my hands behind my back, straining to reach the hook tearing my butt a new one. My right hand finds a thin, leathery thing. "What's this?" I say.

"Your wings," the Frannie look-alike says. "Don't you know you have wings?"

"Wings? Ass goblin wings?"

"Well, they're pink. And a lot bigger than ass goblin wings."

I pull my right hand away, repulsed. "Frannie, is it true? Do I have pink wings?"

Her mouth body frowns. "I'm sorry," she says. "We're all in this together, and at least you don't cough up goblin asses."

"What do you mean *together*?" I point at Frannie 2. "Where are her awful modifications? Why doesn't the White Angel give her pink wings?"

Frannie 2 gets off the floor and walks over to me. She stands below my hanging form. She bends over and spreads her cheeks for me, as if I'm an ass goblin taking roll.

"Stop!" I shout. "Don't do that!"

She wiggles her bottom and the tip of a tongue pokes out. Another few inches of the tongue worms from her buttocks as she gyrates. More and more tongue appears until the tip reaches the floor. A belch from inside of her. No, not a belch. A croak. The croak of a toilet toad.

Frannie 2 nearly splits in half as a toilet toad leaps out of her ass. She drops and convulses on the floor, drooling. A puddle forms around her head like a halo.

The toilet toad stands on its hind legs and waves at me, tongue floating through the air toward my exposed behind. "No! Somebody help!"

"Don't fight the toad," Frannie says. "Your ass needs to be fed. Otherwise it'll get hungry and eat you."

"No, that's not true. Help me."

"The White Angel gave us explicit instructions. I trust him. Even if he mutilated our bodies, he rescued us from Toy Division. He promised that we'll never go back. We're test subjects now."

"I don't want to be a test subjahhhhh!!!" The toad uses its tongue like a retracting pulley and rises into the air, entering me.

Frannie 2 regains consciousness, her face slick with drool. "The toad saves," she says. "The toad saves."

The White Angel barges in. Otto hisses. Everyone else goes silent. Even the toilet toad inside me stops croaking and squirming. A second ass goblin enters the cell long enough to place a stepladder beneath me. The White Angel stands on the top step and grabs hold of me. He yanks my ass off the hook, tearing my flesh and spilling my blubber.

The White Angel sets me on the ground and kicks Frannie 2 across the room. "My toad!" she says. "Give me my toad!"

"Enough about toads," the White Angel says.

"But you said toilet toads are necessary. You told us 999 needed to be cleansed and fed," Frannie 2 says.

The White Angel's eyes extend on their stalks and stretch over to Otto's corner. "Is the spider not getting on with his mates? I thought the four of you were friends. You're two pairs, after all."

Otto raises his front legs as if to attack. He hisses, pressing farther into the corner.

"All in due time," the White Angel says.

I huff and puff, my mouth against the floor. Unlike ass goblins, I have retained my child eyes, so not all is lost. "What do you want with us?" I ask.

The White Angel retracts his eyes from Otto and

smiles. "You're my perfect army."

"Army against who?" Frannie says.

"Darling, don't you know? Adolf can't be gone forever."

An idea congeals in my brain. I assume it sat there for a while before I noticed it. "You did away with Adolf, didn't you? He didn't vanish into thin air."

"We live in a rational universe. Nobody vanishes into thin air. Adolf is interested in two things. He loves ass dolls and wants to rid the earth of children. We all love the dolls, and we're bitter about being born old, with all the miseries and disappointments that age imposes. He wants a childhood. We all do. We've been cheated out of happiness.

"Adolf thinks ass backwards. He refuses to believe that science can deliver childhood to our race. Our golden age will dawn not when children die out, but when we take what we want from children. While Adolf has been away on his sex odyssey, I have made the decision to seize control of Auschwitz. After the four of you destroy him, I can synthesize a childhood serum. Your deaths will give rise to a glorious empire of happy ass goblins."

"What makes you think children are so happy?" Frannie says.

"In your natural habitat, you children live far away from death, in a land of magic."

"Then what gives you the right to make us suffer?" Frannie 2 says.

"You are hybrids. Children will hate you now, and ass goblins have always hated you. Killing Adolf and lending me your childhood are your sole remaining purposes."

"I won't fight for any ass goblin," Frannie 2 says, shaking a fist at the White Angel.

The White Angel kicks her in the tummy and marches out of our cell.

The toilet toad inside me stirs again, tonguing my insides. It doesn't reach for vital organs as it would have in the past. The tonguing actually feels cleansing, like it's gobbling up toxins and other harmful agents. The toad croaks and vomits in my rectum. The puke must be recycled, purified nourishment. It rejuvenates me. Now I see why the ass goblins eat dinner this way, even if it doesn't work with child butts. Toilet toads are the most brilliant solution to starvation and waste management ever. Not that starving was ever a problem when kids were in charge.

"What is a sex odyssey?" I ask.

Frannie and her twin open their mouths, but before they say a word, an ass goblin unlocks the door and wheels in a metal cart piled with cider jugs and a mound of kidskin.

"You're a cannibal," Frannie says. She glares at me through the eyeholes of a greasy face.

I take another swig from a cider jug and shudder as the alcohol leaks into my belly. She pokes her tongue out of the kidskin mouth. "And a Judas," she says.

"You're the one eating the skin of children," I say.

"That's because I have to," she says.

"How is it any different?"

"Eating skin isn't bad because it's necessary for survival. Drinking cider makes you a traitor. It's cannibalism."

I point at Otto. "He's drinking cider too."

"Otto is part spider. He probably doesn't know any better."

The Frannies munch on kidskin in one corner while

Otto and I chug cider in our own corners of the room. Frannie 2 doesn't eat any of the fresh skin. She waits for chunks to fall from the lips of her sister, then sucks on the mushy flesh.

I want to explain to Frannie that mine and Otto's goblin genes must be responsible for our need of cider, but she's all open mouth and closed ears.

Chapter Seventeen

Days sink into other days. Irrelevant in Toy Division, time in the surgery ward melts down to a few minute alterations: when ass goblin sentries change shifts with other ass goblins, skin and cider feasts, the White Angel's visits, and how the four of us adjust to our various mutations.

Otto does pushups around the clock. He gets more buff every hour. Frannie 2 learns to fire the toilet toad out of her ass. It only shoots about halfway across the room, but she practices and improves daily. I am learning to flap my wings, hovering a foot or two in the air. I can also morph into partial S.S. mode, but I'm still overcoming a handicap that purebred ass goblins never encounter: I have eyes on my face. Frannie is worse off than the rest of us. She coughs up goblin asses on the one bed in the room. She boots them away, miserable and disgusted. This is how we pass the time.

I continue to practice Shit Slaughter, learning to widen my mouth and turn my head into a chainsaw of destruction. I am getting better, visualizing ass goblins for some mental target practice. When not doing pushups, Otto broods in his corner.

Twice daily, an ass goblin wheels in a cart of kidskin and cider. The White Angel visits once per day. Of course, I am still a hypocrite and a Judas to Frannie. In her eyes, Otto is now a perfect being, incapable of error.

Chapter Eighteen

The White Angel does not visit us today. For strange reasons I could never explain, I start to miss the barracks, the horrid alarm of morning. Frannie speaks to Otto and her sister, who mutters to herself. No one else speaks to anybody else. The sentries monitor us day in and day out. None of us know morning from night, not without habitual tortures and humiliations to remind us. Something is happening in Auschwitz. I don't know what. Maybe it's the separation from my usual role. The White Angel does not visit us today. That's all I know, for better or for worse.

Chapter Nineteen

A siren screams across the ceiling.

I bury my head in my corner of the room and do my damnedest to ignore its piercing cry, but the tone escalates to pitches that resemble hammers against steel drums. Fogged by exhaustion, I assure myself this must be an error of some type. This screaming must be an error.

The screaming never stops. I stand and stumble over to the viewing window, cupping my ears. I'm ready to fart on the glass or whatever else it takes to convince them to shut off the siren.

No sentries stare in from their quarters. A red light flashes on a white panel bolted above the door leading in and out of the guardroom. Above and below the panel, a luminescent engraving spells F-I-R-E. "Wake up," I yell, unable to hear myself. "Wake up."

But Otto has already stirred from restless sleep and Frannie 2 has poked her head out of Frannie's mouth. They did not have to flatten against the viewing window to see F-I-R-E. They saw it from far away. My vision always makes a fool of me.

"We need to get out of here," I shout. I sense they are shouting the same thing.

I scurry to Otto's corner and unwrap the filthy yellow bandages from his head, seeing why the White Angel forbid us from removing them. Gangrene has spread beneath the rubber mask grafted to his face. The screaming dies a little.

"It must be an air raid," I yell.

He shakes his head to disagree, kind of sad and sickening to look at. The siren dies a little more.

"This is our shot to escape!" I say. I drop some egg-farts.

"Frannie," Frannie mumbles, "can you blast your toilet toad through these walls?"

Frannie 2 shrugs. "I can give it a try."

"Give it a shot."

Frannie 2 crawls all the way out of Frannie's mouth. She sits on her knees, lowers her elbows to the ground for leverage, and raises her ass so that her back arches at a perfect forty-five degree angle. "Count down for me," she says, drooling green saliva.

"Three," I say.

"Two," Otto says.

"One," Frannie says.

Frannie 2 yelps and blasts the toad toward the door. The toad leaves a small four-legged hole. It falls to the floor and twitches. Frannie 2 picks it up and reloads it in her ass.

"Wait," Otto says. He leaves his corner and crawls to the door. He reaches his right front leg through the toad-shaped hole and latches onto the outer door handle. "Locked," he says.

Frannie coughs up a goblin ass. "Stop coughing up asses," I say. "We've got to get out of here."

"I can't help it," she says. She kicks the ass. It sails across the cell and splats *KABOOM!* against the door, blowing it to smithereens.

Otto hisses. One of his front legs twitches in the rubble. He shakes all over and takes off. The rest of us cheer and jet after him, out of the cell.

The alarm blurs the corners of my vision as the four of us run through the flashing hall, searching for any indication of an exit. Otto is swifter than the rest of us. He runs in spirals . . . floor to right wall to ceiling to left wall, leaping and bounding from one surface to another, distancing himself from us slowpokes. "Otto," I say. I can hardly hear myself call his name. I hope his arachnid senses pick up on it. Frannie 2 lags behind. So small and frail, I want to wait for her, but I never fooled myself. I lack the desire to save others. Otto vanishes around a corner to our right.

At the corner, I pause and see that Frannie 2 is having another fit. Frannie holds her down as she foams at the mouth. Behind them, an ass goblin who must have stayed behind opens a door and morphs into Shit Slaughter mode.

I run around the bend, but Otto has left us all behind. Dread pulses through all the pieces of my heart. I turn back.

Frannie hasn't noticed the ass goblin yet. He jiggles his ass behind her, gloating over this easy, unassuming kill. Then he catches sight of me. The goblin points a claw and steps past Frannie and her sister. She never saw the ass goblin coming. At least the goblin doesn't lay a finger on her. It's me he wants. I'm the kid with the pink wings.

I crack my knuckles, pocket my eyes, and transform into Shit Slaughter mode. The only fights I was ever in were against Otto, so a battle against a separate entity is entirely new to me, but after all they've done to us, I'm more than ready to butt heads with a goblin. I refrain from hooting. War cries are a waste of energy if the foe can't hear them.

The ass goblin squares off, fists raised. I wriggle my left claws and make a sudden swipe. The goblin ducks and my hand catches in his crown of teeth. Four fingers on my left hand are ground into dog meat. The pain and sudden blood loss throws my perceptions even more off kilter. The red sirens flutter from black to green and the walls begin to bleed.

I shake it off in time to dodge a wild roundabout punch for my ass. I flap my wings and rise above the ass goblin, dumping a crap on him. He shakes a fist at me, so I flap backwards for a second fly-by shitting. He flaps his tiny wings but quickly realizes that his are no match for my pink furies.

The ass goblin's eyes flash over to the Frannies, where Frannie 2 still convulses. This seizure might kill her even if the ass goblin doesn't tear them both apart. I fart as he lumbers toward them. I fly after the ass goblin. Three feet away, I twist my body and piledrive my butt onto his. The goblin's ass splats like a swollen pimple.

Now to help Frannie and Seizure Girl. My head flips inside-in. Leaving S.S. mode relieves me of an oceanic pressure. Shit Slaughter is a wreck on the nerves. I take my eyes out of my pocket and pop them in place. Frannie nods at me and tucks her twin into her mouth. She runs a lot slower that way, and considering how long the sirens have been blaring, anything might await us outside. This could be the end of Auschwitz.

Back at the bend in the hallway, I notice a silky strand that Otto started. So he never intended to ditch us for good. He may have even gone ahead because he believes his chances of fending off ass goblins or securing the cavern housing Dead Kid Hill are better if he goes alone.

We run down another hallway, following the web strand.

This one ends in a fork, but the strand ends and there's no way of knowing for sure which way leads out of here. Frannie points at the wall between the two passages. A ladder is welded to the wall. I nod. She grabs for the highest rung she can reach and pulls herself up. I follow, uneasy about being on a ladder with all the weight in my lower half, but remember that the ladder is designed for ass goblins. I curl my eye stems upward, fixing my sight on Frannie's lip torso prevent myself from looking down.

The ladder takes us to a field one hundred yards behind the mess hall.

Gunfire and goblin hoots clatter in Auschwitz Square.

I squint at the hazy, swirling desert beyond the field. There are outposts out there, miles away. If we ran for it, they would pick us off. "We've got to get to the bicycle factory," I say. I hope the underground cavern actually leads out of Auschwitz.

The Frannies nod. They know the drill.

Frannie 2 takes my hand and we hurry to the mess hall, sliding along the back of the building and around the corner.

Two apple-shaped spaceships have landed on the apple platter. The ships' stems folds back and ass dolls storm out, swastika-shaped guns jammed in their rectums.

We take off, knowing the ass dolls must have us in their sight. I need to forget that we've got little chance. It's murder to think our flight is hopeless. We scurry as close to the Toy Division factory fronts as possible. To get to the bicycle factory, we have to run by the apple platter's rounded shoulders.

I turn the door of the bicycle factory and find it locked.

Frannie coughs up her twin and with her, a goblin ass. "Get back!" she says. She kicks the goblin ass. On impact, the door explodes into rusted shrapnel.

We step inside, scanning for ass goblins, but the factory is abandoned. I rub my right testicle as we hurry to the guard station door. "What are you doing?" Frannie says.

"Just get the door open!" The bicycle grows inside me.

Frannie 2 pokes her butt out of Frannie's mouth and shoots her toilet toad at the door. The swastika handle goes flying. I get on my bike and turn to Frannie. "Climb on the handlebars and don't let your sister out of your mouth!"

She nods. I pedal into the tunnel.

The added weight of the Frannies makes pedaling difficult, but my legs have grown stronger with my mutations.

The hoots of ass goblins resounding from wherever the green path leads fill the space around me with gelatinous noise-matter. I speed down the yellow path.

I pull out of the second loop . . .

. . . and the third.

The wall of foam bricks has been rebuilt. Frannie wobbles the handlebars, tottering the bike left and right. She screams. Inside her body, her sister screams.

I hit the wall.

She flips over the handlebars and spits Frannie 2 onto the corn road. I sail ass over head after them.

Frannie 2 stares at her hands, disbelieving and coated in her sister's saliva.

"Foam," I say, picking myself up. I toss a brick into

her lap. "The bricks are made of foam."

I help Frannie to her feet. She crouches over her sister and swallows her. "I want to find Otto," she says.

I shake my head *impossible, impossible.* "With dolls and goblins at war? Even if we found him alive, how could we help? He's my brother, not yours. I say we leave him behind."

"You're a Judas," Frannie says.

"I had a chance to leave before, but I resisted because of you and him." In reality, the toads prevented me from leaving. "There is no going back this time. Come on, we've got to move. The toilet toads are around here someplace."

"I won't leave without Otto." She walks in the direction of the green and yellow divide. Frannie 2 waves at me from between Frannie's parted lips.

I plop down cross-legged. "What if Otto is waiting for us on Dead Kid Hill?"

Frannie turns. She says nothing.

"We should at least climb the hill," I say, "then we can decide what's best."

Frannie and Frannie 2 fold their arms.

Maybe I am a Judas.

Frannie caves. I suppose she realizes that I'm not above leaving her. I stand as she walks toward me. "We'll be safe soon," I assure her, maybe the biggest lie I've ever told.

I grab her hand. She growls to let me know that she does not want me touching her.

"I'm scared," I say.

Frannie 2 pokes her head out and says, "You can hold my hand. I don't mind."

I brush her off like a placid nightmare and hike to the

skeletal base of the hill.

Side by side, we walk in darkness. Frannie 2 swipes at my shoulder every so often. I fart to keep her away, regretting the double effect of repelling Frannie.

They gasp when the glowing peak of Dead Kid Hill comes into sight. Depending on the state of decay, the children glow a different color. Most are just skeletons. The ass goblins must have gotten lazy and stopped dragging corpses down here.

Frannie steps in front of me halfway up the hill and turns. Frannie 2 presses her hands against my chest. "We can't go up there," she says.

"We've got to go beyond the hill. This cave might lead us out of Auschwitz," I say. "Besides, we're not little kids anymore. We can handle the toilet toads."

"But this mountain stinks."

"Of course it stinks. It's rotting."

"We'll go back if we don't find Otto," Frannie says.

I shove her hard. She launches Frannie 2 out of her torso and falls on a dead boy whose eyes are still open. Baby cockrats squeal in the sockets. Frannie 2 starts crying. A cockrat, disturbed by her mewing, leaps out of a girl's sunken ribcage and claws at the air, landing on Frannie 2's bald head.

I huff over to her and yank the cockrat from her skull. I fling it off the hill. The creature licks pieces of her scalp from its claws as it sails to the bottom.

"Are you ready to go on?" I say, limping past the Frannies.

Frannie 2 whimpers but nods.

"This was our plan," I say, "and we're sticking to it."

We continue our struggle toward the peak. I really hope we find Otto up there. Otherwise, they'll want to search the green path. I cannot go there with them.

We pass a body who reminds me of 1000. I run my claws along its teeth. A molar pops loose. I wedge the tooth up my asshole.

"Why would you do that?" Frannie says.

"I thought it was someone I knew," I say.

We reach the top of Dead Kid Hill. I look out at the chocolate cake stretching half a mile in every direction. My brother, the spider, is nowhere.

"We've got to go back," Frannie says.

I open my mouth to protest, but someone grabs my shoulder. I try to jerk away, assuming Frannie 2 is making another advance, but the gripper holds me in place.

Spider limbs . . . Otto is here after all. I guess he's always been a little sneaky.

"Otto!" Frannie says.

I wrench away from his furry legs. "Where have you been?"

"I came straight here," he says. "To scout out the cavern."

Frannie dances around him.

"Can we get through?" I say.

Frannie pets his limbs. Otto jerks away, repulsed by her. "I inspected the entire cavern," he says. His gangrenous lips droop into a frown. "The toilet toads are gone, but there's no exit from Auschwitz. This cave is a dead end. I believe we must return and fight."

I'm appalled. "No way," I tell him. I will sooner abandon my friends than fight for my enemies.

"We fight for the children," Otto says.

70

"I'm with Otto," Frannie says.

"Can't we just escape? We'd be able to climb the main gate now. I bet the ass goblins aren't even guarding it." I say this hoping Frannie 2 will side with me. She remains quiet.

"First we fight, then we round up as many children as possible. We can led them out of Auschwitz." He flexes his spider arms. Every tiny hair of his insect-grimy flesh bulges with muscle. His legs slide beneath his torso and shape into a perfect sphere. He's like a bowling pin standing on top of a bowling ball. He yells, levitating in the air as an arachnid sphere.

His upper form—what used to be his torso—melts into a waxen bubble that coats the lower sphere. The wax hardens, forming a protective layer. "Stay here if you want," he says, his voice emanating from the core of his being. "I'm going on. There are goblins to crush."

"Where did you learn that?" I demand.

"Pushups get you far," he says.

"Can we go now?" Frannie says, smooching Otto the Goblin Crusher.

Otto's magical body drops from its levitating position and spins past us. "Come if you want," he says. He rolls down the hill.

Frannie 2 restrains her sister from leaping off the peak. She looks at me and pleads, "Come with us. Look at Otto. He can protect us."

"If he fails?" I say.

"Isn't it better if we die together?"

"Only if death makes all the difference to you." I grab my right testicle and the bicycle sparks into growth.

From the bottom of the hill, Otto hollers for us hurry.

"So what do you think?" Frannie 2 says, struggling to restrain her sister.

Full-sized, the bicycle falls out of me. "You and Frannie take the bike."

"You're not coming?"

"I want to know if my wings can take me down from here."

Frannie slips her sister's clutches. She picks up the bicycle and mounts it. "Let's go!" she says.

Frannie 2 climbs into her mouth.

They careen down the hill the way I did when escaping from the toilet toads, but they aren't evading any danger. They're heading right for it, into the mouth of our killers for a final conflict.

I force myself to forget that escape might be possible if we head straight for the main gate. We'll probably end up Shit Slaughtered for this stupid flight of bravery. I suppose childhood was never anything more than a dream piss that dampened the sheets and dried, but it lingers on as an ammoniac disgust, tainting everything. It's the only thing worth saving. "You're no longer a child," I say to myself. "You have nothing more to lose."

I jump off Dead Kid Hill, flapping my pink furies.

At first, my wings don't hold me up. Corpses swallow everything in my periphery. I rise and flip sideways, eyes scanning the roof high above. Finally, I level out.

We fly or ride or roll to the point where the two roads become one and start down the green trail.

Otto leads since he is virtually a boulder. Swastikas made of apple-scented gelatin drip from the ceiling. I flap harder to catch up with Otto and the Frannies. I cry to the clatter of the bicycle chain as the Frannies plunge after the spider ball. "Wait!"

I fly close to the ground. The green trail is a ninety percent downgrade. Just thinking about the horror show we're stepping into makes me sick. I can't hold back. I vomit.

Otto crashes through something in front of us. The Frannies follow. Ten seconds after them, I flap into a cluster of giant apples that explode into confetti upon impact.

No, not confetti. Toenails and fingernails. The nails of children.

We swerve around corners and up/down turtle-humped dips. Ass goblin laughter grows louder every second. The four of us are approaching something big. I worry that Otto's new ability will be insufficient against the ass goblins, and if we find ourselves in the midst of a brawl between the S.S. and the ass dolls, we are totally doomed.

Otto comes to a sudden stop. Too slow to brake, the Frannies slam into him. Fortunately, his wax layer is still warm and soft enough to lessen the impact. I settle on the path, wings exhausted, and approach the crew.

The Frannies squeeze through a gap on my testicle bicycle. I follow close behind, my wings scraping into Otto's wax armor as I pass between him and the wall. Frannie 2 almost falls into a white, black, green, and red spiral racetrack. We are at the edge of a fifty foot drop.

Rather than leading into another cavern with a hill of bodies and floors of chocolate cake, the green path leads into a moldy labyrinth. I guess this is where they move the cake when it goes bad.

Ass goblins hoot and ride bicycles on the glowing track, zooming through the corridors of mold. Either they don't give a damn that Auschwitz is being invaded, or else they're preparing for war.

"Told you we're screwed," I say.

"I'll kill as many goblins as I can," Otto says. "If they take me down, get out of here. Go help the children."

The entire cavern shakes and Otto slips forward, knocking the Frannies and I off the cliff. We scratch at the air for any object to reunite us with solid land.

I hit the floor, indenting a cake angel into the surface.

Otto leaps off the edge of his own volition as we brush mold and cake from our bodies. Frannie 2 spots my bicycle and prances to its crooked form. She raises the bike and checks for damage. She strokes the ruined brain tires and hugs the skull seat.

"You broke my testicle," I say.

"I'll just ride on the bones," she says.

I gaze around the space we're in. It's kind of a bullpen separated from the actual maze. Otto rolls over to the wall. He is almost the same height as the labyrinth.

"What am I supposed to do?" I say.

Otto rolls over to me, but he doesn't say anything.

While I wait for him to speak, Frannie gobbles her sister and gets on the bike. She rides toward the wall. I look over, too late to stop her. She crashes though it.

Otto tumbles end over end toward the opening left by the bicycle. He destroys a massive section of the wall.

Exhausted as I am, I flap my wings and take to the air. I sway over the labyrinth, swept up by an air current created by the cycling ass goblins. They're all hooting, all in Shit Slaughter mode. On a platform across from the place we fell, the White Angel makes hand and face gestures. He appears to be putting on a drama of some sort. A tragedy, I venture, the way he shoves a fist up his ass.

Chapter Twenty

I fly higher and higher, out of reach, ass-tracking Otto and the Frannies. They're crazy to think riding into this madhouse was a good idea.

I catch sight of Otto. He bulldozes ass goblins by the dozen, but the ones ahead and behind him are catching on. They swarm into sword patterns with other cyclists to pierce Otto's shell. The Frannies are nowhere in sight.

The White Angel ceases his one-goblin play. He skip-skip-hops off the stage and spreads wings identical to mine, only his are white. He soars through the air without flapping.

I worry that Otto might be unaware of the surprise attack, then realize that the White Angel zooms toward me, not him. I go higher.

Hundreds of feet above the labyrinth, the White Angel corners me. It is very silent up here, like my outer space daydreams way back in Kidland.

The White Angel raises his fists. "Where did you learn to fly? That's not in your DNA structure. I installed your wings for purely aesthetic purposes. That way you never forget who your father is."

"Father?" I'm confused. "What is a father?"

"Never mind the father talk. You're an ass goblin. A lousy ass goblin."

"Look at my eyes. My eyes prove I'm a child."

I consider my odds of defeating the White Angel in an aerial battle. A thousand reasons why this is a terrible idea rush through my head, but I see no alternative. I would rather die trying than hit the butcher's block with an apology on my tongue. I guess the others have felt this way all along.

I rake both pairs of claws across the White Angel's belly, catching him off guard. He snaps to, realizing that I'm challenging him to a fight.

The White Angel laughs. He swipes at nothing, mocking me. "Join me," he says.

I swing my ass around and blast the tooth at him. He's too swift for kid tricks and dishes me a playful slap upside the head.

"Join me or be destroyed!" he says, raising his fists again.

Three figures run onto the stage. I point and yell, "Who are they?"

When the White Angel turns, I flap like mad, taking full advantage of this escape opportunity. The White Angel flies in a reverse beeline, hooting and farting. He dives, no longer heading toward the stage. I catch sight of the Frannies. He's narrowing in on them. There is nothing I can do to stop him at this point. He's stronger and already has a huge gain, so I descend and search for Otto. If we're to save the children, we can't all go down at once.

There he is.

I fly low, stirring every nightmare of falling into wakeful alarm. I swoop into the maze between Otto and the goblin pack that threatens to penetrate him from behind.

I barely manage to keep pace with the cyclists, but soon realize a second asset of farting. Farting make you faster. Gas provides that extra *oomph* to make up for clumsy wings.

I descend to within a few feet of Otto. "The White Angel has the Frannies," I yell.

"Go to the stage," he says. "Rescue them and get out of here. Help the children."

"What about you? You can't pin this on me," I say.

"Save them!" he rumbles, sensing the encroaching cycle spears.

I flap out of traffic to the stage. The White Angel twirls out of the labyrinth, wings shimmering. He holds the Frannies and my bicycle in his arms. He takes footing and tosses the Frannies toward the three forms—all of them ass dolls. An ass doll picks up my bike. The two others suction-cuff a Frannie in their lower ass, holding them prisoner.

The White Angel is the first to see me coming. He twists his wings to form a pale umbrella. "Silence!" he cries.

Otto halts in the very center of the labyrinth. Ass goblins hit their brakes. They don't even need to rotate into formation. They've already got him surrounded. Despite his goblin crushing, Otto has ruined everything for all of us. His armor cracked and broken, there are too many ass goblins for him to handle. A thousand brain tires screech, then nothing, no hoots or disgruntled mutterings. In the distance and above, gunfire. Apple gore oozes down the walls.

"Let us go!" the Frannies say, but the moment isn't right to bail them out. Not yet.

The White Angel turns up his palms. "The essence of life is war," he announces. "So what is the value of a life lived and lost in battle?"

"It is the value of toys," the ass goblins say.

"And what do toys bring us?" the White Angel says.

"Toys bring freedom! Toys bring freedom!"

"If toys bring freedom, and war possesses the value of toys, then what is war?"

"War is freedom! War is the essence of life!"

I watch Otto, wondering why he stopped bulldozing goblins. What is he waiting for? Then I catch myself. What am *I* waiting for? Why am I not saving the Frannies? No *right time* exists, not even for the things we must do. If we fail to act—even if we choose the wrong action—we'll be slaughtered like the apples. Otto is absolutely correct. We have to fight. Life isn't about survival. It's about choosing.

"Before the battle proper, we must offer up a sacrifice," the White Angel says. In swirls of rainbow voltage, his wings light up. A green and red swastika blinks off and on amidst purples, oranges, blues, and yellows.

The ass goblins lift their heads and howl, "Adolf! Adolf! Adolf!"

The White Angel spreads his wings. I go Shit Slaughter. Without taking notice of me, he reaches for a lever built into the stage. I run toward him, arms extended. The sole claw of my left hand tears through his wings as they clap together, as he depresses the lever. And the roof retracts.

The underground labyrinth rises. It halts level with Auschwitz Square, destroying all of Toy Division's factories. Swastikles collect on the dead buildings. Children are corralled beside the two ships. They wear swastika blindfolds. Ass dolls stand in a circle around the apple platter, rectal guns raised. Ass goblins ride from the labyrinth, pedaling through icy slush. It is all very theatrical.

I start to back away from the White Angel, but he

catches my hand and pulls me close to him. His face spreads into a jagged grin that shows no pain. It is rounder than the sun.

His breath clouds around my noseless face like rotten, buttered fruit as a third ship—a fraction the size of the other two—zooms out of the fog and lands onstage.

"Someday you will understand why I am this way," the White Angel says.

He tosses me aside and staggers toward the ship. A lone ass goblin steps backwards out of the ship. This ass goblin is naked and has the biggest, most wart-infested ass I have ever seen. Green cheese oozes from eight sausage-length nipples that sag from his sunken chest. All over its body, pimples explode like pus-infused stars. Flies swarm in a crown above its head. Even from a distance and with my poor eyesight, I see its mustache.

"Adolf!" the Frannies scream.

Adolf and the White Angel bow, then engage in a slapping war. After whacking a lot of chocolate cake out of each other, the White Angel and Adolf scoop up handfuls of cake and shove it up the other's ass. They embrace. This must be how ass goblin leaders shake hands.

"Adolf," the White Angel announces. "With these mutant inheritors of Auschwitz, I welcome you back from your sex odyssey. Without further adieu, may we witness how they play in combat?"

"Intolerable, despicable," Adolf says.

The White Angel ruffles his wings. He gestures toward me. "What seems to be the problem? That child is half ass goblin."

Having been absent during our transformative days, Adolf appears angry and bewildered. We are not the children he used to murder, not anymore. "I see the ass goblins have degenerated into weak, stupid creatures in my time away."

"They have always been stupid," the White Angel says. "Given half a chance, my prototypes will provide a bridge to even stronger, purer ass goblins. And when we venture on, they will ensure that Auschwitz becomes more brutal, filled with more toys."

"We will see about your mutants . . . in a three-way battle!" Adolf flails his arms and stomps his feet. "I declare, my stupid, loving slaves, it shall be the ass goblins versus the ass dolls versus the children! The strong must earn the chair they sit on if they want to drink at my table. No more fucking toy business! No more fucking freedom killings! The final conflict has begun!"

Despite being unsure what *fucking* means, I understand Adolf's message. And I decide I've heard enough. I scramble for the Frannies. Mesmerized by Adolf, the ass dolls restraining them fail to notice me. I uppercut one of them and follow with a left hook to the other. My arm sinks into her upper ass. The first doll springs to her feet. I rip my arm free and yell at the Frannies to move. The dead dolls' rectums slacken enough for the Frannies to pull free. I never wanted to pick this battle, but it's too late. I'm here, squaring off with a doll who must die.

She scissor kicks and misses. Frannie 2 steps between the ass doll and I. She bends over, twisting her butt in front of the doll. When the ass doll reaches for her, the toilet toad pokes out of Frannie 2's rectum and coils its tongue around the midsection between the doll's two asses. The doll falls in half.

Frannie 2 grabs hold of my wings, throwing me off balance as a figure waddles toward me. Before I can react,

Adolf clocks me in the jaw. I stagger and swoon over the edge of the stage. He throws a few more punches but none of them connect. I hopscotch sideways along the cliff until I regain my balance. Frannie 2 slips and falls. "Wahhh!" she screams.

The White Angel tackles Adolf and smothers him beneath his ass. He poops on Adolf's mustache. Adolf starts to yell in protest, but then breaks into laughter. He rakes his claws through his mustache, smearing the bile. "Fucking kill! Kill for freedom!"

Frannie looks terrified, but she manages to crawl in my direction. I scoop her in my arms and flap my pink furies. As we descend, I remain as close to the stage as possible. Below us, the dolls and goblins battle. They're drunk on war, emitting fouler odors than ever before. Hopefully Otto can fend them off.

We reach ground level, the ruins of Toy Division, as the Shit Slaughterers pedal forth. Barbwire ropes fly out of their bicycles. The ropes coil between the dual asses of dolls and slice them in half.

The ass dolls spread into a half circle, each firing two rectal guns. The heads and asses of Shit Slaughterers explode. These ass dolls are cutting down the cyclists like it's target practice. A few children remove their blindfolds and attempt to flee, but they're cut down. The others fall to their knees and bow their heads. They've been submissive so long, they forgot how to rebel or act for themselves.

In the midst of this disaster, Frannie 2 has little chance of surviving. "Come on," I say, taking Frannie by the hand. She lets me this time. We're going to find her sister.

I turn my head for a second, long enough to see the ass dolls cutting down another cluster of Shit Slaughterers.

Frannie trips over a headless goblin. Without losing a step, I scoop her onto her feet. Frannie 2 yelps nearby. We scan the crumbling structures, searching out nooks where she might have tucked away. She cries out a second time, sounding much closer. I look down and there she is, trapped beneath the ass goblin Frannie tripped over. I can't believe we missed her. I roll the goblin to the side and take both Frannies in my arms, then *FLAPPPPPPPPP*. We rise over the battlefield, taking in all the action. The goblins and dolls no longer seem interested in them. Instead, they gang together to attack Otto. He bowls over them like a pinball, but they shoot and bite and claw at his shield, relying on sheer numbers. Onstage, Adolf and the White Angel pull instruments out of their asses and play to the hoots and death gargles.

"The children! The children!" Frannie 2 says.

"We've got to help Otto," Frannie cries, and despite the pounding in my skull and the dark sun looming big and for once hopeful overhead, I know she's right.

But Otto is my brother, and if he were in my shoes, he would save the kids. Because he is my brother, I'll try to do as he would. I veer toward the circle of children . . . .

Chapter Twenty-One

Dead Kid Hill rises, spewing molten chocolate cake and toilet toads like a volcano. The Frannies, my sirens, shriek. I loop backwards and down.

An ass doll shoots me out of the sky. The bullets tear swastika-shaped holes in my wings, driving me into a spiral toward Auschwitz Square. In their frantic attempts to hold on, the Frannies tear my wings off.

I fall into cold swastikle mush. Frannie hits the ground near my head. Frannie 2 follows, landing on her head near my feet. She convulses worse than ever. Frannie crawls to her side and pins her shoulders to the slush. She looks up at me and says, "Go help Otto." She swallows her sister.

My wing stumps bleed, warming my back. Otto heads in our direction, followed by dolls and goblins. I scramble toward the cluster of children.

The Frannies and I slip the blindfolds from their heads. Soon, hundreds of eyes watch us. I'm unsure if they're more frightened or bewildered. "Get up!" I yell.

Over one hundred children stand. Most kids already died. It's the ones who are jaded to the carnage, who stood awaiting orders, that survived. Although we no longer re-semble them, the children realize we're trying to help. Some of them even pick up cockrats scuttling by and wield them as weapons. They look to me for orders. Unsure about the best course of action, I look behind me. Otto has reversed his path. He rolls away from the mixed platoon of dolls and goblins and speeds toward a cluster of goblins on bikes. He's a speedball of furious intent. He's offering us a chance to lead the kids to the gate.

Frannie opens her mouth and her sister hops inside. They point at the stage. The White Angel is tracking him, weaving and bobbing. Adolf clings to his back, firing swastika bullets at falling toads.

Frannie 2 squeezes out of Frannie's mouth and screams, "Roll, Otto, roll!"

Adolf aims the gun at Otto as I turn back to the kids. I take a boy and a girl by their hands and walk in the direction of the gate. The others understand, and follow. Frannie runs to my side. "What about Otto?" she says.

"Think of the children," I tell her. "This is what he wanted."

As we pass the ruins of Toy Division, Dead Kid Hill rains chocolate cake and toilet toads. The toads crawl around, seeking asses to plug.

"Frannie 2?" I say.

"Yes?" she says.

"Can I have your toilet toad?"

"Of course!" She twists around in her sister's mouth until her ass pokes out. She releases the toad in a mist of diarrhea. I bend over. It hops and slips and slides into my rectum, immunizing me against other toilet toads.

A gang of dolls climbs out from a pile of rubble that used to be the doll factory. I release the girl and boy and form scissor hands. The dolls flank us, six in all. "Keep moving, no matter what," I tell the two children.

I charge the ass dolls, moving my arms like scissors. None have guns. I slice all six in half and twelve asses quiver in the snow.

Kids in the back of the group scream. A lone ass goblin speeds after us on a super tall bike. Barbed ropes swing from the handlebars. Frannie 2 throws a goblin ass out of her sister's mouth and tosses it to the ground. Frannie kicks it, but the ass sails wide to the left, blowing up dead dolls instead. There's no time for me to get there, but I rush toward the goblin anyway.

A dark-haired skeleton of a girl steps away from the mass. She swings a cockrat by the tail. The goblin veers toward her. She winds up and releases the cockrat. The disgruntled, starving creature gnashes at swastikles and lands right in the ass goblin's jaws. Instead of being shit slaughtered, the cockrat starts eating the teeth of the goblin. He rides the bike straight into a deepening pool of hot cake.

The girl takes two cockrats from the nearest children in possession and locks eyes with me. She waves her vermin-holding hands at the group, indicating that if I guard the right side, she will guard the left. I give her a thumbs up since my thumb is the only appendage remaining on my left hand. "Take the rear!" I shout to the Frannies.

I search the skies for Adolf and the White Angel. Otto battles them onstage. He's returning to spider goblin form, no longer the impenetrable boulder. Dead Kid Hill ceases flowing cake and toads. And lying amidst the ruins, ass goblins plug ass dolls while toilet toads plug every open rectum.

Ahead of the girl and boy, above the main gate of Auschwitz, a neon sign beats back the darkness. It tells us that toys bring freedom.

Chapter Twenty-Two

Beyond the gates, white orbs of snow overtake the swastikles. Frannie 2 crawls out of her sisters mouth. She stands between us, taking Frannie's right hand and my bleeding left stump. Every piece of my heart beats faster, throbbing what feels like nine hundred and ninety-nine times every minute. We have done what we set out to do, but there's no place in the pure and silent land for us.

The dark-haired girl pushes through the children. She holds the cockrats at her side, indifferent to their teeth and claws.

She stands in front of us, then turns to the girl and boy. "We can't live the way we used to," she says. She swings the cockrats. They latch onto the faces of the two children, driving them into the gate.

The girl turns to us. "Are you going to open the gate or what?" she says.

I look to the Frannies, finding blank expressions. Then Frannie coughs up a goblin ass. She kicks the ass at the lock. It explodes, and the letters T-O-Y come unhinged from the gate, crashing into the snow on the other side.

The girl steps very close to me. She is even tinier up close. Her forehead comes up to my waist. She stretches her hand out. I offer her my right hand. We shake. I guess things will be different now. The end of Auschwitz doesn't nullify the fact that it happened. Everyone left alive will have to sift through the ashes and find where to start again.

She opens the gate and yells at the children to file through. None of us ask where they're heading. Nobody needs to. They leave Auschwitz single-file, stepping over the dead boy and dead girl. After the last of them goes, Frannie 2 tries to follow. I move to block her. Frannie steps to my side. "We don't belong out there," she says, pointing to the land beyond Auschwitz.

Although we are not free, and we will never leave Auschwitz, I am glad to know we're on the same page again.

"What if Otto is dead?" Frannie 2 says.

"Adolf and the White Angel must die," I say, "so that someday Kidland can be rebuilt."

"But we can help rebuild it!"

Frannie smacks her lips disapprovingly. "We aren't children anymore. We're products of Auschwitz, we're freaks. We can never live in a society of children again."

Frannie closes the gate and takes my good hand. I offer my left thumb to Frannie 2. Together, we face Auschwitz. We march toward Dead Kid Hill and the ruins of Toy Division. "I know it sounds terrible," I say, "but right now this kind of feels like home."

Frannie's torso widens into a smile.

In Auschwitz Square, the morning siren screams.

ABOUT THE AUTHOR

Cameron Pierce is the author of *Shark Hunting in Paradise Garden* and the creator of Meat Magick, a squid-smashing performance series. He lives in a bunker with other bizarro authors and artists in Portland, Oregon. You can write to him at CameronCPierce@gmail.com.

Bizarro books

Bizarro Books publishes under the following imprints:

www.rawdogscreamingpress.com

www.eraserheadpress.com

www.afterbirthbooks.com

www.swallowdownpress.com

For all your Bizarro needs visit:

WWW.BIZARROCENTRAL.COM

Introduce yourselves to the bizarro genre and all of its authors with the Bizarro Starter Kit series. Each volume features short novels and short stories by ten of the leading bizarro authors, designed to give you a perfect sampling of the genre for only $5 plus shipping.

BB-0X1
"The Bizarro Starter Kit"
(Orange)

Featuring D. Harlan Wilson, Carlton Mellick III, Jeremy Robert Johnson, Kevin L Donihe, Gina Ranalli, Andre Duza, Vincent W. Sakowski, Steve Beard, John Edward Lawson, and Bruce Taylor.

236 pages $5

BB-0X2
"The Bizarro Starter Kit"
(Blue)

Featuring Ray Fracalossy, Jeremy C. Shipp, Jordan Krall, Mykle Hansen, Andersen Prunty, Eckhard Gerdes, Bradley Sands, Steve Aylett, Christian TeBordo, and Tony Rauch.

244 pages $5

BB-001 "The Kafka Effekt" D. Harlan Wilson - A collection of forty-four irreal short stories loosely written in the vein of Franz Kafka, with more than a pinch of William S. Burroughs sprinkled on top. **211 pages $14**

BB-002 "Satan Burger" Carlton Mellick III - The cult novel that put Carlton Mellick III on the map ... Six punks get jobs at a fast food restaurant owned by the devil in a city violently overpopulated by surreal alien cultures. **236 pages $14**

BB-003 "Some Things Are Better Left Unplugged" Vincent Sakwoski - Join The Man and his Nemesis, the obese tabby, for a nightmare roller coaster ride into this postmodern fantasy. **152 pages $10**

BB-004 "Shall We Gather At the Garden?" Kevin L Donihe - Donihe's Debut novel. Midgets take over the world, The Church of Lionel Richie vs. The Church of the Byrds, plant porn and more! **244 pages $14**

BB-005 "Razor Wire Pubic Hair" Carlton Mellick III - A genderless humandildo is purchased by a razor dominatrix and brought into her nightmarish world of bizarre sex and mutilation. **176 pages $11**

BB-006 "Stranger on the Loose" D. Harlan Wilson - The fiction of Wilson's 2nd collection is planted in the soil of normalcy, but what grows out of that soil is a dark, witty, otherworldly jungle... **228 pages $14**

BB-007 "The Baby Jesus Butt Plug" Carlton Mellick III - Using clones of the Baby Jesus for anal sex will be the hip sex fetish of the future. **92 pages $10**

BB-008 "Fishyfleshed" Carlton Mellick III - The world of the past is an illogical flatland lacking in dimension and color, a sick-scape of crispy squid people wandering the desert for no apparent reason. **260 pages $14**

BB-009 "Dead Bitch Army" Andre Duza - Step into a world filled with racist teenagers, cannibals, 100 warped Uncle Sams, automobiles with razor-sharp teeth, living graffiti, and a pissed-off zombie bitch out for revenge. **344 pages $16**

BB-010 "The Menstruating Mall" Carlton Mellick III - "The Breakfast Club meets Chopping Mall as directed by David Lynch." - Brian Keene **212 pages $12**

BB-011 "Angel Dust Apocalypse" Jeremy Robert Johnson - Meth-heads, man-made monsters, and murderous Neo-Nazis. "Seriously amazing short stories..." - Chuck Palahniuk, author of Fight Club **184 pages $11**

BB-012 "Ocean of Lard" Kevin L Donihe / Carlton Mellick III - A parody of those old Choose Your Own Adventure kid's books about some very odd pirates sailing on a sea made of animal fat. **176 pages $12**

BB-013 "Last Burn in Hell" John Edward Lawson - From his lurid angst-affair with a lesbian music diva to his ascendance as unlikely pop icon the one constant for Kenrick Brimley, official state prison gigolo, is he's got no clue what he's doing. **172 pages $14**

BB-014 "Tangerinephant" Kevin Dole 2 - TV-obsessed aliens have abducted Michael Tangerinephant in this bizarro combination of science fiction, satire, and surrealism. **164 pages $11**

BB-015 "Foop!" Chris Genoa - Strange happenings are going on at Dactyl, Inc, the world's first and only time travel tourism company.
"A surreal pie in the face!" - Christopher Moore **300 pages $14**

BB-016 "Spider Pie" Alyssa Sturgill - A one-way trip down a rabbit hole inhabited by sexual deviants and friendly monsters, fairytale beginnings and hideous endings. **104 pages $11**

BB-017 "The Unauthorized Woman" Efrem Emerson - Enter the world of the inner freak, a landscape populated by the pre-dead and morticioners, by cockroaches and 300-lb robots. **104 pages $11**

BB-018 "Fugue XXIX" Forrest Aguirre - Tales from the fringe of speculative literary fiction where innovative minds dream up the future's uncharted territories while mining forgotten treasures of the past. **220 pages $16**

BB-019 "Pocket Full of Loose Razorblades" John Edward Lawson - A collection of dark bizarro stories. From a giant rectum to a foot-fungus factory to a girl with a biforked tongue. **190 pages $13**

BB-020 "Punk Land" Carlton Mellick III - In the punk version of Heaven, the anarchist utopia is threatened by corporate fascism and only Goblin, Mortician's sperm, and a blue-mohawked female assassin named Shark Girl can stop them. **284 pages $15**

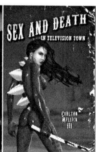

BB-021"Pseudo-City" D. Harlan Wilson - Pseudo-City exposes what waits in the bathroom stall, under the manhole cover and in the corporate boardroom, all in a way that can only be described as mind-bogglingly irreal. **220 pages $16**

BB-022 "Kafka's Uncle and Other Strange Tales" Bruce Taylor - Anslenot and his giant tarantula (tormentor? fri-end?) wander a desecrated world in this novel and collection of stories from Mr. Magic Realism Himself. **348 pages $17**

BB-023 "Sex and Death In Television Town" Carlton Mellick III - In the old west, a gang of hermaphrodite gunslingers take refuge from a demon plague in Telos: a town where its citizens have televisions instead of heads. **184 pages $12**

BB-024 "It Came From Below The Belt" Bradley Sands - What can Grover Goldstein do when his severed, sentient penis forces him to return to high school and help it win the presidential election? **204 pages $13**

BB-025 "Sick: An Anthology of Illness" John Lawson, editor - These Sick stories are horrendous and hilarious dissections of creative minds on the scalpel's edge. **296 pages $16**

BB-026 "Tempting Disaster" John Lawson, editor - A shocking and alluring anthology from the fringe that examines our culture's obsession with taboos. **260 pages $16**

BB-027 "Siren Promised" Jeremy Robert Johnson - Nominated for the Bram Stoker Award. A potent mix of bad drugs, bad dreams, brutal bad guys, and surreal/incredible art by Alan M. Clark. **190 pages $13**

BB-028 "Chemical Gardens" Gina Ranalli - Ro and punk band Green is the Enemy find Kreepkins, a surfer-dude warlock, a vengeful demon, and a Metal Priestess in their way as they try to escape an underground nightmare. **188 pages $13**

 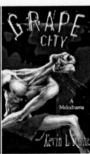  

BB-029 "Jesus Freaks" Andre Duza - For God so loved the world that he gave his only two begotten sons… and a few million zombies. **400 pages $16**

BB-030 "Grape City" Kevin L. Donihe - More Donihe-style comedic bizarro about a demon named Charles who is forced to work a minimum wage job on Earth after Hell goes out of business. **108 pages $10**

BB-031"Sea of the Patchwork Cats" Carlton Mellick III - A quiet dreamlike tale set in the ashes of the human race. For Mellick enthusiasts who also adore The Twilight Zone. **112 pages $10**

BB-032 "Extinction Journals" Jeremy Robert Johnson - An uncanny voyage across a newly nuclear America where one man must confront the problems associated with loneliness, insane dieties, radiation, love, and an ever-evolving cockroach suit with a mind of its own. **104 pages $10**

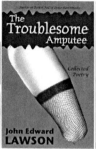

BB-033 **"Meat Puppet Cabaret" Steve Beard** - At last! The secret connection between Jack the Ripper and Princess Diana's death revealed! **240 pages $16 / $30**

BB-034 **"The Greatest Fucking Moment in Sports" Kevin L. Donihe** - In the tradition of the surreal anti-sitcom Get A Life comes a tale of triumph and agape love from the master of comedic bizarro. **108 pages $10**

BB-035 **"The Troublesome Amputee" John Edward Lawson** - Disturbing verse from a man who truly believes nothing is sacred and intends to prove it. **104 pages $9**

BB-036 **"Deity" Vic Mudd** - God (who doesn't like to be called "God") comes down to a typical, suburban, Ohio family for a little vacation—but it doesn't turn out to be as relaxing as He had hoped it would be... **168 pages $12**

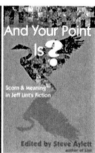

BB-037 **"The Haunted Vagina" Carlton Mellick III** - It's difficult to love a woman whose vagina is a gateway to the world of the dead. **132 pages $10**

BB-038 **"Tales from the Vinegar Wasteland" Ray Fracalossy** - Witness: a man is slowly losing his face, a neighbor who periodically screams out for no apparent reason, and a house with a room that doesn't actually exist. **240 pages $14**

BB-039 **"Suicide Girls in the Afterlife" Gina Ranalli** - After Pogue commits suicide, she unexpectedly finds herself an unwilling "guest" at a hotel in the Afterlife, where she meets a group of bizarre characters, including a goth Satan, a hippie Jesus, and an alien-human hybrid. **100 pages $9**

BB-040 **"And Your Point Is?" Steve Aylett** - In this follow-up to LINT multiple authors provide critical commentary and essays about Jeff Lint's mind-bending literature. **104 pages $11**

BB-041 **"Not Quite One of the Boys" Vincent Sakowski** - While drug-dealer Maxi drinks with Dante in purgatory, God and Satan play a little tri-level chess and do a little bargaining over his business partner, Vinnie, who is still left on earth. **220 pages $14**

BB-042 **"Teeth and Tongue Landscape" Carlton Mellick III** - On a planet made out of meat, a socially-obsessive monophobic man tries to find his place amongst the strange creatures and communities that he comes across. **110 pages $10**

BB-043 **"War Slut" Carlton Mellick III** - Part "1984," part "Waiting for Godot," and part action horror video game adaptation of John Carpenter's "The Thing." **116 pages $10**

BB-044 **"All Encompassing Trip" Nicole Del Sesto** - In a world where coffee is no longer available, the only television shows are reality TV re-runs, and the animals are talking back, Nikki, Amber and a singing Coyote in a do-rag are out to restore the light **308 pages $15**

BB-045 **"Dr. Identity" D. Harlan Wilson** - Follow the Dystopian Duo on a killing spree of epic proportions through the irreal postcapitalist city of Bliptown where time ticks sideways, artificial Bug-Eyed Monsters punish citizens for consumer-capitalist lethargy, and ultraviolence is as essential as a daily multivitamin. **208 pages $15**

BB-046 **"The Million-Year Centipede" Eckhard Gerdes** - Wakelin, frontman for 'The Hinge,' wrote a poem so prophetic that to ignore it dooms a person to drown in blood. **130 pages $12**

BB-047 **"Sausagey Santa" Carlton Mellick III** - A bizarro Christmas tale featuring Santa as a piratey mutant with a body made of sausages. 124 pages $10

BB-048 **"Misadventures in a Thumbnail Universe" Vincent Sakowski** - Dive deep into the surreal and satirical realms of neo-classical Blender Fiction, filled with television shoes and flesh-filled skies. **120 pages $10**

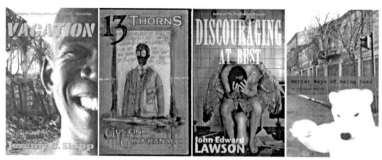

BB-049 **"Vacation" Jeremy C. Shipp** - Blueblood Bernard Johnson leaved his boring life behind to go on The Vacation, a year-long corporate sponsored odyssey. But instead of seeing the world, Bernard is captured by terrorists, becomes a key figure in secret drug wars, and, worse, doesn't once miss his secure American Dream. **160 pages $14**

BB-051 **"13 Thorns" Gina Ranalli** - Thirteen tales of twisted, bizarro horror. **240 pages $13**

BB-050 **"Discouraging at Best" John Edward Lawson** - A collection where the absurdity of the mundane expands exponentially creating a tidal wave that sweeps reason away. For those who enjoy satire, bizarro, or a good old-fashioned slap to the senses. **208 pages $15**

BB-052 **"Better Ways of Being Dead" Christian TeBordo** - In this class, the students have to keep one palm down on the table at all times, and listen to lectures about a panda who speaks Chinese. **216 pages $14**

BB-053 **"Ballad of a Slow Poisoner" Andrew Goldfarb** Millford Mutterwurst sat down on a Tuesday to take his afternoon tea, and made the unpleasant discovery that his elbows were becoming flatter. **128 pages $10**

BB-054 **"Wall of Kiss" Gina Ranalli** - A woman... A wall... Sometimes love blooms in the strangest of places. **108 pages $9**

BB-055 **"HELP! A Bear is Eating Me" Mykle Hansen** - The bizarro, heartwarming, magical tale of poor planning, hubris and severe blood loss... **150 pages $11**

BB-056 **"Piecemeal June" Jordan Krall** - A man falls in love with a living sex doll, but with love comes danger when her creator comes after her with crab-squid assassins. **90 pages $9**

BB-057 "Laredo" Tony Rauch - Dreamlike, surreal stories by Tony Rauch. 180 pages $12

BB-058 "The Overwhelming Urge" Andersen Prunty - A collection of bizarro tales by Andersen Prunty. 150 pages $11

BB-059 "Adolf in Wonderland" Carlton Mellick III - A dreamlike adventure that takes a young descendant of Adolf Hitler's design and sends him down the rabbit hole into a world of imperfection and disorder. 180 pages $11

BB-060 "Super Cell Anemia" Duncan B. Barlow - "Unrelentingly bizarre and mysterious, unsettling in all the right ways..." - Brian Evenson. 180 pages $12

BB-061 "Ultra Fuckers" Carlton Mellick III - Absurdist suburban horror about a couple who enter an upper middle class gated community but can't find their way out. 108 pages $9

BB-062 "House of Houses" Kevin L. Donihe - An odd man wants to marry his house. Unfortunately, all of the houses in the world collapse at the same time in the Great House Holocaust. Now he must travel to House Heaven to find his departed fiancee. 172 pages $11

BB-063 "Necro Sex Machine" Andre Duza - The Dead Bicth returns in this follow-up to the bizarro zombie epic Dead Bitch Army. 400 pages $16

BB-064 "Squid Pulp Blues" Jordan Krall - In these three bizarro-noir novellas, the reader is thrown into a world of murderers, drugs made from squid parts, deformed gun-toting veterans, and a mischievous apocalyptic donkey. 204 pages $12

BB-065 "Jack and Mr. Grin" Andersen Prunty - "When Mr. Grin calls you can hear a smile in his voice. Not a warm and friendly smile, but the kind that seizes your spine in fear. You don't need to pay your phone bill to hear it. That smile is in every line of Prunty's prose." - Tom Bradley. 208 pages $12

BB-066 "Cybernetrix" Carlton Mellick III - What would you do if your normal everyday world was slowly mutating into the video game world from Tron? 212 pages $12

BB-067 "Lemur" Tom Bradley - Spencer Sproul is a would-be serial-killing bus boy who can't manage to murder, injure, or even scare anybody. However, there are other ways to do damage to far more people and do it legally... 120 pages $12

BB-068 "Cocoon of Terror" Jason Earls - Decapitated corpses...a sculpture of terror...Zelian's masterpiece, his Cocoon of Terror, will trigger a supernatural disaster for everyone on Earth. 196 pages $14

BB-069 "Mother Puncher" Gina Ranalli - The world has become tragically over-populated and now the government strongly opposes procreation. Ed is employed by the government as a mother-puncher. He doesn't relish his job, but he knows it has to be done and he knows he's the best one to do it. 120 pages $9

BB-070 "My Landlady the Lobotomist" Eckhard Gerdes - The brains of past tenants line the shelves of my boarding house, soaking in a mysterious elixir. One more slip-up and the landlady might just add my frontal lobe to her collection. 116 pages $12

BB-071 "CPR for Dummies" Mickey Z. - This hilarious freakshow at the world's end is the fragmented, sobering debut novel by acclaimed nonfiction author Mickey Z. 216 pages $14

BB-072 "Zerostrata" Andersen Prunty - Hansel Nothing lives in a tree house, suffers from memory loss, has a very eccentric family, and falls in love with a woman who runs naked through the woods every night. 144 pages $11

BB-073 **"The Egg Man" Carlton Mellick III** - It is a world where humans reproduce like insects. Children are the property of corporations, and having an enormous ten-foot brain implanted into your skull is a grotesque sexual fetish. Mellick's industrial urban dystopia is one of his darkest and grittiest to date. **184 pages $11**

BB-074 **"Shark Hunting in Paradise Garden" Cameron Pierce** - A group of strange humanoid religious fanatics travel back in time to the Garden of Eden to discover it is invested with hundreds of giant flying maneating sharks. **150 pages $10**

BB-075 **"Apeshit" Carlton Mellick III** - Friday the 13th meets Visitor Q. Six hipster teens go to a cabin in the woods inhabited by a deformed killer. An incredibly fucked-up parody of B-horror movies with a bizarro slant. **192 pages $12**

BB-076 **"Rampaging Fuckers of Everything on the Crazy Shitting Planet of the Vomit At smosphere" Mykle Hansen** - 3 bizarro satires. Monster Cocks, Journey to the Center of Agnes Cuddlebottom, and Crazy Shitting Planet. **228 pages $12**

BB-077 **"The Kissing Bug" Daniel Scott Buck** - In the tradition of Roald Dahl, Tim Burton, and Edward Gorey, comes this bizarro anti-war children's story about a bohemian conenose kissing bug who falls in love with a human woman. **116 pages $10**

BB-078 **"MachoPoni" Lotus Rose** - It's My Little Pony... *Bizarro* style! A long time ago Poniworld was split in two. On one side of the Jagged Line is the Pastel Kingdom, a magical land of music, parties, and positivity. On the other side of the Jagged Line is Dark Kingdom inhabited by an army of undead ponies. **148 pages $11**

BB-079 **"The Faggiest Vampire" Carlton Mellick III** - A Roald Dahl-esque children's story about two faggy vampires who partake in a mustache competition to find out which one is truly the faggiest. **104 pages $10**

BB-080 **"Sky Tongues" Gina Ranalli** - The autobiography of Sky Tongues, the biracial hermaphrodite actress with tongues for fingers. Follow her strange life story as she rises from freak to fame. **204 pages $12**

BB-081 **"Washer Mouth" Kevin L. Donihe** - A washing machine becomes human and pursues his dream of meeting his favorite soap opera star. **244 pages $11**

BB-082 **"Shatnerquake" Jeff Burk** - All of the characters ever played by William Shatner are suddenly sucked into our world. Their mission: hunt down and destroy the real William Shatner. **100 pages $10**

BB-083 **"The Cannibals of Candyland" Carlton Mellick III** - There exists a race of cannibals that are made of candy. They live in an underground world made out of candy. One man has dedicated his life to killing them all. **170 pages $11**

BB-084 **"Slub Glub in the Weird World of the Weeping Willows" Andrew Goldfarb** - The charming tale of a blue glob named Slub Glub who helps the weeping willows whose tears are flooding the earth. There are also hyenas, ghosts, and a voodoo priest **100 pages $10**

COMING SOON

"Fistful of Feet" by Jordan Krall
"Cursed" by Jeremy C. Shipp
"Warrior Wolf Women of the Wasteland"
by Carlton Mellick III
"The Kobold Wizard's Dildo of Enlightenment +2"
by Carlton Mellick III

ORDER FORM

TITLES	QTY	PRICE	TOTAL

Please make checks and moneyorders payable to ROSE O'KEEFE / BIZARRO BOOKS in U.S. funds only. Please don't send bad checks! Allow 2-6 weeks for delivery. International orders may take longer. If you'd like to pay online via PAYPAL.COM, send payments to publisher@eraserheadpress.com.

SHIPPING: US ORDERS - $2 for the first book, $1 for each additional book. For priority shipping, add an additional $4. INT'L ORDERS - $5 for the first book, $3 for each additional book. Add an additional $5 per book for global priority shipping.

Send payment to:

BIZARRO BOOKS
  C/O Rose O'Keefe
  205 NE Bryant
  Portland, OR 97211

Address			
City		State	Zip
Email		Phone	

CPSIA information can be obtained at www.ICGtesting.com
Printed in the USA
BVOW040058151112

305634BV00001B/14/P